among
monsters

ALSO BY JAMIE MCGUIRE

PROVIDENCE (PROVIDENCE TRILOGY BOOK ONE)

REQUIEM (PROVIDENCE TRILOGY BOOK TWO)

EDEN (PROVIDENCE TRILOGY BOOK THREE)

BEAUTIFUL DISASTER

WALKING DISASTER

A BEAUTIFUL WEDDING (A BEAUTIFUL DISASTER NOVELLA)

BEAUTIFUL OBLIVION

RED HILL

AMONG MONSTERS

HAPPENSTANCE: A NOVELLA SERIES

HAPPENSTANCE: A NOVELLA SERIES (PART TWO)

APOLONIA

among monsters

JAMIE McGUIRE

ISBN-13: 978-1502937537

For Heather Summers

contents

chapter
one

REGRET WASN'T SOMETHING a thirteen-year-old thought about much. Lashing out or making a bad choice would typically be forgiven the moment the mistake was recognized, and then it would be forgotten. With volleyball, cheer squad, student council, piano lessons, and the occasional spare moment for a social life, there wasn't much time for anything else, definitely not something as stupid as regret. But when all of that fell away, that was all I would be thinking about.

When I got out of Mom's Suburban that morning, my thoughts swirled around what snotty comment Ally or Lizzie would say to me that day or if I would get all the way through lunch without a single crap remark. Math homework was due. Dad would be picking me up this afternoon.

Dad.

Ugh.

Mom had mentioned being nice to his new girlfriend, but I wasn't even sure who that might be. Ever since the divorce, Dad's house had been a revolving door of single moms or women who were barely older than me.

At first, Dad had tried to control how much and how seriously Mom dated by example. His first girlfriend had her own kids, and she hadn't come over much on the weekends when my little sister, Halle, and I were there. But after Dad had realized Mom wasn't interested in dating—and he couldn't hold his rules over her head—he'd quit caring. Girlfriend number two had broken us in, and he had felt okay with the idea of her being around us. By number three, he'd been just fine with her spending the night. He'd introduced us to Four thirty-six hours after their first date. Five had a toddler son, and Dad had moved my things out of my bedroom to make space for blue-and-red curtains, fire truck wall hangings, and a toy box full of dump trucks and miniature cars. Six had barely been old enough to drink and didn't have kids, and even though my bedroom had become empty again, I was still stuck sharing a room with my seven-year-old sister.

Now, we were on Seven, so it was possible that my room was back to being occupied.

I slipped inside the glass double doors of Bishop Middle School without glancing back to see if Mom had pulled away. She always waited until I was at the doors. She probably didn't even realize that she did it anymore.

The sky opened up, and large drops began to spatter against the windows. The tapping seemed to echo throughout the building as I walked up the stairs to the main floor. I turned left, heading toward my locker, and passed Mrs. Gizzo on the way.

She smiled brightly at me. "Just made it! Looking wet out there already," she said.

I nodded.

"See you later." She winked before passing me by.

Mrs. Gizzo taught my third-hour seventh grade English class. She didn't mind when I'd write stories in class as long as my work was finished. Writing was pretty much the only outlet I had. Talking to Mom about being angry or frustrated with her wasn't exactly happening. Talking to her about Dad would only cause a fight. Mrs. Gizzo had somehow gotten that about me, and she wouldn't give me a hard time about getting the anger out of my system on paper like some of the other teachers had.

I stopped in front of my locker and turned the combination lock to four, forty-four, twelve. I pulled the handle with a jerk and opened the thin metal door before pulling out my pre-algebra book and then stuffing my backpack inside. I had spent too much time on my laptop the night before, so my math homework would have to be finished during homeroom.

My cell phone buzzed in my back pocket, and I turned my body to hide the bulky teal-and-purple case as I checked the message. It was from Dad, reminding me that he would be picking me up.

I'm not an idiot.

I typed back that I was aware, and then I shoved my phone back into my pocket.

"Hey, Jenna!" Chloe said with a big grin.

I jumped. "Hey."

Her smile faded. "Is it your dad's weekend?"

"Yeah," I said, pulling my thick binder from my locker.

"That sucks. Well, maybe he'll feel bad about last time and take you someplace fun."

"Doubtful. Seven will likely be around."

Chloe's face screwed into disgust. "They have numbers now?"

"Might as well." I exhaled, walking with her to homeroom.

When Chloe and I sat in our seats, I immediately pulled out the crinkled notebook paper bookmarking the page of problems I had to finish. Just ten minutes and four problems later, I folded my work in half and stuck it in my textbook.

Mr. Hilterbran was tapping on his cell phone while resting his chin on the heel of his other hand. I frowned, and motioned to Chloe. It was unlike him—or any teacher—to have a phone in view of the students. Seeing Mr. Hilterbran breaking the rules by ignoring us for whatever was on his phone was strangely unsettling.

Chloe leaned over. "He's been like that since he sat down."

Five minutes before the bell rang, Mr. Hilterbran seemed to snap out of his trance, and he blinked. "Have you heard about this epidemic in Europe?" he asked. "It's all over the news."

The twenty or so of us looked at each other and then stared blankly at our teacher. He simply looked back down at his phone and then shook his head in disbelief.

"What kind of epidemic?" I asked.

Mr. Hilterbran began to speak, but the bell rang. I gathered my things and waited while Chloe made a quick stop at her locker before going on to pre-algebra.

Chloe and I had all but one class together. Last hour, she had choir, and I had volleyball.

As we climbed the stairs to the second floor, Chloe grimaced. "Have you ever noticed all the smells in the stairway?"

Chloe's bright red highlights peeked out from her chestnut hair. We used to look more alike, but her mom was a hairstylist, and since we'd started middle school, Chloe's hair had become much more interesting than mine.

I waited for her always-thoughtful opinion. Her mind worked in the most puzzling and wonderful way, which was one of the many things I found so endearing about her. She was quiet unless she had something philosophical to say.

"Like perfume, BO, cologne, and mildew. The higher we climb, the worse it gets."

"It's the humidity," I said.

She shook her head. "Maybe it's the stairway telling us what to expect—like, every year, we'll all be more defined as individuals. The stereotypes will just get stronger each year until we graduate."

"Or maybe it's just the humidity," I said, smiling.

Just when we entered Mrs. Siders's room, she held up her hand, signaling us to be quiet while she worked on hooking up the Smart Board cables to her laptop.

As more students came in, the murmur and chatter grew louder.

Mrs. Siders swept back a curly piece of long hair that had escaped her loose low bun. "Please! Quiet!" she said as we found our seats.

After a live feed of the national news began to play, Mrs. Siders took a few steps back and hugged her middle with both arms. I watched her, knowing that the teachers would never intentionally let on that they were afraid, so she probably didn't realize she was even doing it. That made me worry even more.

Mrs. Siders shook her head as the bell rang.

I trained my eyes on the anchorman detailing the chaos displayed in the small square beside his head. Yellow words trailed across the bottom of the screen, listing countries.

"What's going on with those countries?" Tryston said. He had just walked in, late as usual.

"They're the countries that the UN has lost contact with," Mrs. Siders said.

I frowned. "What do you mean? How is it possible to lose contact with an *entire* country?" I asked.

Mrs. Siders didn't turn around. "The Prime Minister of France just declared a state of emergency. In the last half an hour, the UK has reported cases of the virus, and they said it's spreading uncontrollably."

"Should we be watching this?" Tryston swallowed, his barely burgeoning Adam's apple bobbing.

"Would you like for me to turn it off?" Mrs. Siders asked.

"It's kind of scary," Morgan squeaked from the back of the room.

"Not as scary as not knowing what's happening," I said. "We should leave it on."

We watched the same channel for the duration of class. No one talked. Once in a while someone would gasp or sigh to remind me where I was.

Germany had been the first to go. The countries to the north, like Norway and Sweden, hadn't been heard from since half past eight. France had gone quickly, and then Spain, Italy, England, Ireland, and Greece had all reported cases.

An amateur video with a cell phone flashed for just a few seconds. The anchorman blanched, and I felt sick to my stomach. People were running from something with absolute terror on their faces, but we couldn't see what they were running from.

"It won't cross the ocean, right?" Tryston asked.

"Right," Mrs. Siders said.

As she glanced back at our class, I could see the worry in her eyes. When she turned back around, I texted my dad.

Are you watching the news?

Yes. How are you?

Worried.

It'll be fine. Gov. Bellmon just rolled into town. He wouldn't have come if he were worried about it.

K.

Love you. See you soon.

Chloe fidgeted. "I heard on the radio this morning something about a scientist and dead people in Germany. The news lady said they were trying to neutralize the cadavers, but my mom said that didn't make any sense. I think it makes perfect sense. The Bible says the dead in Christ shall rise, you know. It also says that whosoever eats of Christ's flesh and drinks of his blood shall live eternally."

"That's gross, Chloe."

She sighed. "And yet so poetic."

I pushed my phone back into my pocket and looked over to my friend. "My dad says the governor is in Anderson for some kind of photo op with the firefighters. I doubt he'd be going through with a fundraiser if the government was worried about an epidemic."

Concern weighed down Chloe's usually bright and cheerful expression. "You don't think it's possible…the dead coming back and attacking the living?"

"No," I said, shaking my head.

"Sounds like freakin' zombies," Tryston said.

First, a collective gasp sucked the air out of the room, and then everyone erupted into panicked chatter.

"Can we call our parents?" one of the girls asked.

"I'm calling my mom!" another girl said.

"Okay, guys," Mrs. Siders said, holding up her hands, palms out. "No cases have been reported in the US yet. Let's all just calm down. Take a deep breath. The school will keep a close eye on this, and if we hear of a reason to worry, they'll dismiss everyone. Until that happens, there's no point in getting upset."

The bell buzzed, and we gathered our things. With Chloe just behind me, I rushed down the stairs and put my things in my locker. Chloe did the same, one section down, and we reconvened to head to second hour.

"Come get me!" a girl shrieked into her phone. "I don't care! Come get me right now, Daddy!"

The principal and vice principal were manning the halls with grave expressions on their faces.

"I have a bad feeling," Chloe said. "When you hear about war or whatever on the news, it doesn't feel real. It's over there, ya know? It doesn't feel in your face. This feels close."

"Too close," I said.

chapter two

THE HALLS WERE EERILY QUIET. If the kids spoke at all, it was in whispers, as if speaking of their fears too loudly would make them real.

Chloe and I walked downstairs where there were radioactive signs that I hadn't paid much attention to before that moment. Bishop Middle School was a designated fallout shelter since before my grandparents were born and could supposedly withstand tornadoes and anything else that might come our way—except for a fast-spreading virus. Plus, being underground made me feel trapped, not safe.

Mom and I were apocalypse junkies, and we would watch end-of-the-world prep shows. It was kind of our thing. We'd even been to a couple of conventions. I wondered if Mom had the same red flags going up as I did. Something deep and inherent was screaming for me to run even though I didn't know where to run or from what I should be running.

I pulled out my phone to text her.

Chloe set her books down on her desk two rows behind me. Mr. Holland hadn't allowed us to choose our own seats in the beginning of the semester like Mrs. Siders had. He didn't have a Smart Board in his room either.

"Okay, put your phones away," Mr. Holland said. "I know a lot is going on in the world right now, but it's not going on here. Until Principal Hall announces dismissal, we'll go on as usual. *Capisce?*"

The entire classroom argued, but Mr. Holland won out, insisting we open our books and at least pretend to concentrate on the lesson. I put my phone away and opened my textbook to page two hundred forty-nine as instructed.

Pretend was exactly what we had to do, and most of the kids in that room failed miserably. Carina Tesh began to sniffle, and by the time the bell rang, her whimpering had prompted tears from several girls in the classroom.

As Chloe and I ascended the stairs to the main level, we saw through the large glass doors and windows of the school entrance the many cars parked at the curb, and adults and kids were running in or out of the school.

"Where's your mom today?" I asked.

Chloe pressed her lips together. "She went down to Greenville. She had to pick up some things. She'll be back by the time school is out though."

"Maybe she'll come back early."

Chloe's eyes fell to the floor. We both knew Greenville was far enough away that her mom would be lucky to make it back by the last bell.

After lunch, the classrooms were half empty.

In history class, Mrs. Stuckey had her Smart Board hooked up as well. A graphic that read *Breaking News* rolled on and then off the screen, and the news anchor appeared with a deep line between his brows.

"I'm Brian Jenkins, and welcome back to KFOR. We've just received word that the first cases of an unknown virus have hit US soil. Atlanta and New York City airports are both reporting chaos as the infected are attacking travelers in the terminals."

"No. Dear Lord, no," Mrs. Stuckey said before covering her mouth.

Without caring about the consequences, everyone pulled out their phones and began tapping text messages. Some even made phone calls, screeching at their parents about the news.

I texted my dad.

> *Please tell me you're on your way.*

> *Yes. Picking up your sister from the grade school now. Will be there soon. Sit tight.*

I put my phone away. Chloe bit her lip, fingering her phone.

"If my dad gets here before you get a hold of her, you can come with us."

She shook her head. "I can't go to Anderson. My mom would freak out."

"Maybe we could drop you off at your house then?"

Chloe frowned at her phone. "She'll be here."

By the next hour, Chloe and I were two of only six kids in Spanish class. A seventh-grader walked in with several pieces of paper and handed them to Mrs. Hall. With heavy eyes, she looked across her mostly empty classroom.

"Cole, Tanner, Amelia, Addison, and Jenna, your parents are here to pick you up."

Everyone but me scrambled to gather their things, and they rushed out the door.

Chloe waved good-bye to me. "I'll text you later."

"Are you sure you don't want to come with us?" I asked.

She shook her head, and a contrived smile stretched across her face. "I'll wait for my mom. Get going. I bet Halle is freaking out in the car."

"Okay. Text me as soon as she picks you up."

"Later, tater," she said, trying to keep the tremble from her voice.

I didn't stop by my locker. Chloe was right. If Dad had to come into the school to check me out, Halle would be in the car alone and likely working herself up into a frenzy.

Dad stood out in his dress blues, holding his hat under his arm. It was the first time he'd come to pick me up while wearing his formal clothes, and for a moment, it made me forget why he was here early.

"Wow," I said.

He looked like a soldier instead of a firefighter.

"Let's go," Dad responded. He guided me out the door and down the steps with a hand on my shoulder.

His white Chevy Tahoe was still running with the windows rolled up when we reached his place in line. Halle wasn't panicked at all when I opened the front passenger door. She was sitting behind me in the middle row in one of the two captain's chairs with her seat belt fastened and her hands folded tightly in her lap. The back bench seat had a case of bottled waters and several white plastic sacks full of cans.

After climbing into my seat, I put my textbook and binder on the floorboard. "Hey, Halle," I said, trying to sound cheerful. I turned around to smile at her only briefly before buckling in.

Dad jumped into his seat and pulled the gear into drive. Pulling away from the curb, he asked, "You buckled in, Pop Can?"

He wasn't talking to me. One of the other firefighters had once said that Halle was no bigger than a pop can, and it had stuck. Born five weeks early, she was pretty small for her age. She had worn toddler-sized clothes until she was in kindergarten. Dad was half an inch shorter than Mom, so we always teased Halle for being petite like him. Dad didn't find that funny, so he stayed with Pop Can.

Halle tugged on her seat belt and then wiped her nose with the back of her hand.

Dad rounded a corner quickly, and my shoulder bounced off the door.

"Sorry. I'm trying to get out of town. How was your day?" Dad asked with a tinge of nervousness in his voice.

I raised an eyebrow at him. "What's wrong with Halle? Why is she being so quiet?"

"Some of the parents came into the school, causing a fuss. She's still upset." He kept his eyes on the road.

"Did you tell Mom you were picking us up early?"

"I called the hospital. I couldn't get through."

"Did you call her cell phone?" I asked.

He made a face. "She doesn't like it when I call her cell phone when she's at work. She said to only do it when it's an emergency."

"An epidemic isn't an emergency?"

"If I call her cell phone, she'll think something happened to one of you. I'm not going to scare her. Your grandma said she called her, and your mom was in surgery. I'm sure she'll call when she can."

I pulled out my phone and began to type out a text.

"What are you doing?" Dad snapped.

"I'm at least going to let her know where we are and that we're okay."

"Put it away, Jenna. I told you, she's in surgery. I don't want to hear it from her later."

"She said I could text her if it's important."

"Do you want her to think you're hurt?"

I huffed and looked out the window. I watched the buildings slowly spread out until there was only farmland and refineries. We passed over the interstate toward the toll road, and I was about to ask Dad where he was going, but it didn't take long for me to figure it out. The traffic both north and south on I-35 was still flowing, but I'd never seen it that busy before. Dad was probably going to Anderson from the south through the old Tempton highway.

Within fifteen minutes, Dad turned north, confirming my suspicion. Another fifteen minutes later, we were in Anderson's city limits. We passed the high school and the baseball fields, the fairgrounds, and then downtown.

"Where are we going?" I asked.

I glanced back at Halle. She still hadn't said a word, which was completely abnormal. She usually barely took a breath when we were in the car and fighting for airtime.

"To the armory," he answered.

"Still?" I asked. "I was kind of hoping we'd go home and watch the news."

"Why do you think I've left the radio off?" he said. "It's not a good idea." He peeked at the rearview mirror and winked at Halle. "No need to scare your sister."

"She's already scared."

He turned right at the northeast corner of town. Three blocks before the armory, the parking lots of the surrounding buildings were nearly full. The haphazard parking and packed lots looked like the fairgrounds would during fair week, but we were on the wrong side of town.

"There's so many cars," I said.

"A lot more than when I left," Dad said.

"All these people have come to the armory because they think it's safer to be near Governor Bellmon, don't they?"

"He's called in the National Guard just to be safe," Dad said. "They should be here soon."

"I'm not sure if that's comforting or not."

Dad patted my leg. "It's just a precaution. I won't let anything happen to you. Hear that, Halle? You're with Daddy. Nothin' to worry about."

Halle didn't answer.

Dad found a parking spot, and we each held one of Halle's hands as we crossed the busy street. It seemed the whole county was driving toward the armory. Dad took us in through the armory's back entrance, and we found a group of firefighters looking formal in their dress blues. Dad joined them, blending in.

"Hey, kiddo," Jason Sneed said with a wink. He was blond, blue-eyed, young, and charming.

I'd had a crush on him since I was four. I'd even told him once that I was going to marry him one day, and I'd believed it until he'd gotten engaged two years later.

"Hey," I replied.

"You doing okay?" he said quietly.

"So far. Heard anything new?" I asked.

"It's spread along the East Coast. But we're in the middle of nowhere. Nothing ever comes this far. The military is containing it. Governor Bellmon is in contact with some US senators, and they're confident."

"That's what he's saying anyway," I grumbled.

Jason narrowed his eyes, but his small smile betrayed him. "So young yet so cynical."

The governor was elevated above the crowd on a makeshift stage in the center of the room, speaking comforting words into a microphone, as people yelled questions and concerns.

"I hear what you're saying. I'm not saying not to worry. With words like *epidemic* and now *pandemic* being thrown around…it's a worrisome situation. But we're safe here, and that's what we need to focus on now. Panic won't solve anything."

"Is it the terrorists?" someone yelled.

"No," the governor said, amused. "I've been told it's a virus."

"What kind of virus?" someone else asked.

"We're not exactly sure yet," Governor Bellmon said.

He was being honest. I'd give him that.

"There are reports in Mississippi!" a man said, holding up his phone.

The crowd erupted, and the governor leaned over to whisper something in a man's ear. He was dressed in a suit, and he nodded before leaving the stage immediately. He walked over to Tom, the fire chief, just feet away from where we stood. Tom listened intently to the man in the suit and then waved to his men to come closer.

"The governor has ordered we gather water and supplies. We're going into disaster mode, guys. I know most of you came in for the photo op, but you're getting called in. Let's get going."

The men gave a nod and turned for the back door. Dad looked around and caught Tom as he was making his way toward the police chief and the mayor.

"Tom, I've got my little girls here," Dad said.

Tom looked down at Halle and me and then nodded, giving Dad an unspoken pass, before he continued on.

"Now what?" I asked.

"We wait for the guys to get back and help as best as we can." He leaned in, whispering in my ear, "Do me a favor, Jenna. Stay off your phone. I don't want any of the stuff on the news to scare your sister."

I felt a small hand grip mine. I knelt down beside Halle. Her stringy blonde hair was a ratty mess as it always was after school. Her clothes were mismatched, and her heather-gray hoodie jacket was tied around her waist. She pushed up her black-rimmed glasses, her ice-blue eyes glistening.

We couldn't look more different—Halle with her light-blue eyes and tiny frame and me with my honey-brown irises and chestnut hair. I was always athletic, always pushing against boundaries, vying for independence, even when I was little. Halle just always seemed so fragile.

As if she could hear my thoughts and personify them, she squeaked her next words, "I want Mom."

"I bet she'll head this way as soon as she gets off work. She'll want to be here with us," I said.

Halle shook her head. "She won't come here, Jenna. She'll go to our place."

"Red Hill? That's just if something bad happens, silly."

Halle looked around at the roomful of frightened people. "This is bad, Jenna."

I stood and squeezed her to my side.

chapter
three

THE CONCRETE WALLS AND FLOOR OF THE ARMORY seemed so much smaller than when I had been here for the National Guard's open house the year before. It was just one giant room, but even back then, when the huge military vehicles had been parked inside, the space had seemed bigger. Now, the vehicles were parked outside, but with so many people packed inside, it made me feel a little claustrophobic. Still, as the news reports worsened and the news that the governor was in Anderson, more people were finding their way to the aging brick building.

Dad was helping the other firefighters pass out water and blankets, and they were also plugging in fans to every outlet they could find. Governor Bellmon was standing on the stage, speaking words of comfort, while holding out his hands between moments of wiping the sweat dripping from his brow. He looked like a doomsday preacher during an outdoor revival, only we were crammed inside a run-down building that was older than my dad.

I couldn't imagine how hard it was to be responsible for keeping so many people calm in such a frightening situation. I was glad it was him and not me.

"I can't breathe," Halle said.

Her moist skin made her glasses slip down her nose so often that she'd resorted to pushing them atop her head like Mom would do with her sunglasses. When she tried to focus, her left eye would turn in.

I patted her nose with the bottom of my blouse and lowered her glasses in place. "Your crazy eye isn't behaving," I said with a wink.

Being premature, Halle had been sick a lot as a child. Mom had said that Halle coming early explained why she was the only one with glasses in our immediate family and why she was so much smaller than everyone in her class. Mom would also insist that Halle was as strong as any of us and to definitely never, ever give Halle a complex about her lazy eye. Mom would say all of this while babying Halle, of course. But when her glasses or lazy eye were mentioned, we would rarely make a big deal about it, and if we did, it was to proclaim how weird it was that one of her classmates had even noticed. We'd call it her crazy eye instead.

Halle pulled her mouth to the side. "I'm hungry."

I led her over to a table with laundry baskets full of snack food. I picked out four small bags of potato chips and put four bottles of water in Halle's backpack. We walked together through a rickety wooden door to a grassy yard surrounded by a tall fence, the ominous kind with curly barbed wire on top. A few rusted Humvees and military trucks were parked there. I even noticed a tank that I was sure was just for show.

Some of the other townspeople were grouped together, discussing theories on the origin of the virus and making phone calls. Halle picked out a spot in the corner of the yard, and we sat down in the grass, already green from the overabundance of spring rain.

Just as I thought about texting Chloe, Halle hopped up. "My pants are wet!"

I jumped up, too, checking my backside for the inevitable damp spot. I sighed. "Sorry. I'll find something for us to sit on."

I walked back into the armory and found several packages of plastic table covers. I took a package and opened it with my teeth while rejoining Halle outside.

"Here," I said, spreading the plastic on the ground. "Our own little picnic."

"I'm cold," Halle whined.

"It's cooling off," I agreed. "And you were sweating inside. That'll make you colder faster."

She untied the sleeves of her jacket wrapped around her waist and put it on. "Sweat will?" she asked, confused.

I shrugged and zipped up her jacket. "That's kind of the point."

Halle munched on her chips as we watched more vehicles drive down Sixth Street. The drivers seemed to be searching for places to park.

"Why are so many people coming here?"

"Probably because the governor is here, and they think it must be safe."

"Is it?"

"I don't know," I said. "The cops and firefighters are here, and the National Guard is coming. I'd say we're safer than most."

That brought Halle a moment of comfort, but it only lasted a few seconds before she frowned again. "I want Mom."

I pressed my lips together. "Me, too."

Several young men in hunter's camouflage came through the wooden door and out to the yard, yelling at people to get back inside the armory. I grabbed Halle and pulled her out of the way before wadding up our tablecloth and stuffing it into her backpack.

Dad's voice called our names from inside, and then he appeared, rushing over to us. "Where have you been?" he said, angry.

"Halle was hungry," I said.

His attention was already on the men. Some of them were starting up the Humvees, and others were opening the oversized gate at the end of the yard.

"What are they doing?" I asked.

Dad turned away from Halle and spoke softly, "There are reports of the virus in our state. The National Guard isn't coming. The governor gave those guys permission to take the military vehicles to the roads running in and out of town to make sure no one who's infected gets in."

Women and children began to cry. Voices got much louder as the Humvees pulled out of the gate, and the young men chained it shut again. Other men rushed to their own trucks, heading to the highways leading out of town.

"Have you called Mom yet?" I asked. "What about Mom? Did you tell them to let her in?"

Dad was in a deep conversation with Tom.

"Dad? Dad!"

"Not now, Jenna."

"Have you talked to Mom?" I said, unrelenting.

He stopped his conversation, breathed out a controlled but frustrated sigh, and shook his head. "Your grandma said she talked to your mom earlier. She was still in surgery. She's busy."

I pulled out my phone. It was almost time for her to get off work. Chloe had been out of school for over an hour, and she hadn't texted me yet.

"I'm calling her."

"Jenna, don't."

"I'm calling her!"

Halle lifted her glasses and wiped her eyes before watching me. I touched the screen and then held the phone to my ear. A series of beeps came through the speaker. I tried again.

"Can't get through?" Dad asked, unable to hide the alarm in his voice.

Once the beeps started again, I hit End. "You should have let me try earlier!"

"Jenna, calm down," Dad said.

I tried texting Chloe. A minute passed, and then a little red icon popped up next to my message showing that it hadn't gone through. After a brief moment of panic, I noticed the worried look on Halle's face, so I swallowed back my fear.

Dad put his hand on my shoulder. "She'll be here, Jenna. This is the first place she'll come when she leaves the hospital."

I held Halle against my side. "Hear that? We'll see her in an hour or two."

Halle touched her forehead to my stomach and shook her head.

I knelt down, waiting until Halle's eyes met mine. "She will, and she won't let anything stop her."

Halle hugged me, and Dad hugged us both before coaxing us back into the building. Instantly, the air was hot and stale. The tension was thicker, and Halle felt it, too. Something twinged in my chest as she squeezed my hand tight.

The governor wiped his brow with a handkerchief and then shoved it back into his breast pocket. "We've got three dozen men on patrol. They're experienced hunters or marksmen. Rest assured that we've got Anderson locked down."

"I've got family who are trying to get home!" a woman shouted.

After more yelling, the governor motioned for everyone to settle down. "The infection has spread to our state. If they're not infected, they'll be allowed in. But I've heard several reports that the interstate has shut down."

The crowd exploded again.

I clicked on my phone to check the time. Mom should be halfway to Anderson by now.

Commotion from the yard interrupted the shouting citizens inside. Several people rushed out to see what it was, and then more yelling ensued. The door was left open, and a series of popping noises, like fireworks, echoed from down the road.

"Stay here," Dad said, leaving us just inside the door before stepping out into the yard.

"What is that?"

"Is that gunfire?"

"The boys are shooting!"

"What are they shooting at?"

Wailing weaved together and formed a symphony of fear and anguish. It was stifling and stuffy inside the building and chilly outside. The sun was lower in the sky, and I knew it would only get colder.

"Dad?" I said when he returned. "Do we have to stay here?"

"The chief wants us here while people are choosing to stay here."

"I didn't bring my coat."

"You've got one at the house." He patted my back while looking past me to warily scan the yard.

"Halle only has her jacket. Maybe we should go to the house and get some of our things?"

He nodded. "We will."

"I don't want to spend the night here."

"Me either," Halle whimpered.

Dad glanced around the room. "People are getting sick fast. It's probably not a good idea to be in here with all these people."

I agreed.

"Tom," Dad called his chief over.

Tom shouldered past several people to get to us. He always seemed fairly devoid of emotion, except for the occasional chuckle. His voice was monotone, but his eyes were kind. He didn't stand much taller than my dad's five feet nine inches, but being the chief, he didn't scare easily. In that moment though, fear flashed in his eyes.

"Have you heard from either of your girls?" Dad asked.

Tom shook his head, looking a little lost. "Nope," he sighed. "Connie's phone quit working about an hour ago. They were both trying to get home from college, and they were taking the interstate. I'd told them that would be the fastest route home coming from Greenville."

Dad made a face. "They're together?"

"Always."

"They'll take care of each other," Dad said, glancing at Halle and me.

Tom showed a moment of appreciation and then looked around. "This group isn't going to stay calm for long. We'll need everyone ready to help the police when the panic starts."

"I wanted to talk to you about that. I was hoping to take the girls home. Maybe we should instruct everyone to go home. It doesn't seem safe, having everyone grouped together like this, when an infection is spreading fast."

"I said the same," he said quietly. "The governor instructed the police to keep everyone here. They just went outside to get their rifles and gear."

"Christ, that's going to make it worse."

"I know it. They know it. The governor is just doing the best he can, and they're following orders."

"What the hell does the governor know about riot control?" Dad growled.

Tom put a hand on Dad's shoulder. "Not a damn thing."

Dad stiffened. "They can't force us to stay here."

"I don't think they'll shoot ya, but you've got to stay, Andy. It's your job to help these people."

"I'm a father first, Tom."

Tom looked down at Halle and me with a sympathetic expression. "We've all got a job to do. You do what you think is right."

He walked away, and Dad watched him, his jaw moving beneath his skin.

I checked my phone again for the time and for any messages from Mom or Chloe. *Nothing.*

"Is she almost here?" Halle asked.

"Almost," I said, not sure if I was telling the truth.

The brakes of a military truck squeaked in the street near the armory's entrance, and then more people came in through the front doors.

"Are they giving people rides?" Halle asked.

One of the gunmen shoved a father forward, and his frightened wife and sons followed.

"Back off!" the father growled, pulling his wife and kids under his arms.

"I'm not sure that's what they're doing," I said.

"My Lord, it is hot, hot, hot," a nearby woman said, dabbing the forehead of her young son. Her long braids were wrapped in a bun on top of her head, and she held her son's red puffy coat over her other arm.

"I want to go home, Mommy," the boy said around the finger in his mouth.

"I know you do, baby. Me, too." Her eyes brightened when she saw Halle. "There's a little girl. Maybe she'll play choo-choo with you." She walked over to us. "Hi there."

"Hi," Halle said.

With one hand, the boy held tightly on to his mother's leg. His hair was freshly trimmed, and his smooth mocha skin was a stark contrast against his white tee. He looked to be around four or five.

The mother batted his other hand away from his mouth. "What do you say, son?"

He held out his hand. "I'm Tobin. Nice to meet you."

Halle looked up at me. Tobin's finger was still glistening with his spit.

Halle would collect tiny bottles of hand sanitizer and not just because it was the new thing at school. She had started the trend. Not only was Halle a borderline germophobe, she was also a hoarder. Dad had even dubbed her second backpack a B.O.C.— Bag of Crap. She would keep tiny toys from McDonald's Happy Meals, an old camera, a calculator that hadn't worked in years, three or four notebooks and several pens, and random items she'd collected from toy machines at stores or restaurants. Once, I'd even found a coagulated bottle of nail polish that had to have been as old as she was.

"Gross!" the mother said, chuckling. She took a sanitizer wipe from Tobin's preschooler-sized backpack and rubbed his fingers and palms.

Halle waited a few seconds until his hand was dry, and then she took it. "Halle."

The boy ripped off his backpack and sat on the floor before pulling out small cars and a few miniature trains. Halle sat down with him and watched for a moment before joining in. She was twice his age, but she still liked a good playdate.

"I'm Tavia," the woman said, crossing her arms across her stomach, as she watched the little kids play.

"Jenna." I was sure that my smile was awkward. It felt strange to have such an ordinary conversation when the armory was slowly being turned into an internment camp.

"You doing okay?" Tavia asked.

"Today is pretty messed up," I said.

She laughed at my honesty. "Where are your parents?" She dabbed her brow with the heel of her hand.

"My dad's over there," I said, tossing my head in his direction. He was helping his shift partner organize medical supplies in the corner of the room. "My mom works in Bishop. She's on her way here."

"Oh," she said, suddenly concerned. "My brother is on his way here, too. I haven't heard from him in several hours though. I heard the interstate is gridlocked. Did you hear that?" she asked.

"Earlier, yes."

"I have a confession," Tavia said, keeping her voice low. "I knew your dad was one of the firefighters. I figured you might have overheard something useful."

"Just that I-35 is closed down, and the police want us all to stay here."

Just as I uttered the words, several men in riot gear came through the large double doors we'd come through, holding semiautomatic rifles. A collective gasp traveled from the entrance to where we stood, and the crowd began to panic again.

Governor Bellmon stood on his perch. "Now, this is just a precaution. Emotions are running high. It's going to get dark soon. We want to make sure all safeguards are in place before the sun goes down. That's all. Everyone, try to remain calm."

Tavia laughed once without humor. "Remain calm? That man's done lost his damn mind."

"It's a stressful time. He's just doing his best," a man snapped.

Tavia turned around. "I'm not saying he's not. He's always taken care of our state. But he should let us do our best at home. Just sayin'."

The corners of my mouth turned up. I liked her.

"The sun is going to set soon." Halle pushed up her glasses as she looked up at me.

Tobin banged his train car into hers, pretending that the driver or passengers or whoever were screaming—quietly, of course.

"They brought back flashlights and candles," I said.

Tavia leaned back to get a better look at the far wall. "I see some tall work lights over there, several of 'em. I'd say they're prepared—at least for the night."

"Are we staying here?" Halle asked, her voice going up an octave. "I don't wanna stay here."

Tavia leaned in. "Me either, but I bet it's just for one night. They'll get this mess figured out, and then we can all go home."

I was glad Tavia had replied for me. Halle often asked a lot of questions I wouldn't know the answers to. I wouldn't feel too bad though. Neither Mom nor Dad would know all the answers either.

I looked over at my dad. In that moment, he happened to glance over to check on us, and our eyes connected. He was trying to hide it, but I could see that this was one of those times he didn't know the answer. I wondered if anyone did.

IT HAD JUST BEGUN TO QUIET DOWN when someone began to beat on the entrance doors. A few police officers unfastened the chains they had wrapped around the door handles an hour earlier.

An older man in camo burst through. "They've...they've killed them! The stupid sons-a-bitches gunned them all down!"

People gasped, and the crying began again.

"Who?" the police chief said, standing between the man and the crowd.

"Those idiots guarding the overpass! They gunned down a truck and then an entire family trying to pass through—"

"What family?" someone asked.

The panicked chatter ignited.

"I don't know. I tried to stop them. I tried to stop them!" the man said. He began to cry. "Then, the people stuck in traffic below...they got out of their cars and tried to run into Anderson. Those boys gunned everyone down! They're all dead! Men...women...kids...the boys shot everyone who moved."

The yelling and screaming got louder.

"What do we do?"

"Why would they do that?"

"Is the infection here?"

"It's here! The infection is here! They wouldn't just shoot innocent people!"

"No! No!" the older man said. "They weren't infected!"

"Now, you don't know that," Governor Bellmon said, his voice booming. "Let's work on the assumption that they have successfully protected us. Please! Please calm down!"

"Protected us? What if the people out there were our families trying to get home?" a man yelled.

A woman cried out, and fists rose in the air as people demanded answers.

"We can't leave!" the governor shouted. "We don't know the whys of what happened, but we know people are being killed out there. If you want to live, you must stay in here!" He gathered himself and then spoke more softly, "We all know what this is. We must stay together."

The panic and sobbing quieted to whimpers and humming conversations.

Dad walked over and knelt next to Halle. "Doing okay, Pop Can?"

He would only call her that when he was trying to lighten the mood. She hadn't caught on to it yet, but I'd figured it out right after the divorce. Dad would get excessively weird when he was trying hard to play dad. It was more natural for him to play a skirt-chasing firefighter.

Halle sniffed.

Dad noticed Tavia and Tobin when he stood.

"My son wanted to play with your girl. Hope that's okay."

"Yeah," Dad said, dismissively waving her away. "Thank you. She needs the distraction, too."

"I'm Tavia. This is Tobin," she said, indifferent that her son wasn't concerned with introductions.

"Andrew," Dad said, shaking her hand. The gray crowding his brown hair above his ears caught the light just right. In that moment, he looked a lot older—or maybe it was from the burden of fear he was holding inside.

Tavia's polite smile faded. "He's wrong—the governor. It's not safe to lock this many people inside a building with only two exits. If something goes wrong—"

"It won't," Dad said, glancing at Halle and me.

Tavia ignored him. "Your girls will notice. If something ugly comes through those doors and we're all trying to squeeze through that one, they'll notice. No sense in trying to keep it from them when it's just down the street."

Dad took a step toward her. "You heard Bellmon. He said to stay in here, and the police department is going to enforce his demand."

Tavia repositioned her stance. She wasn't the type to back down. It reminded me of the hundreds of power struggles Dad had fought and lost with Mom. That was why they'd gotten a divorce. She never let him win, not even when it hadn't mattered. He always said it took a special kind of man to marry a redhead. It had turned out that he wasn't it. On the days when I was on the losing end of one of her tirades, I couldn't blame him for when he'd stopped trying.

"I have a son," Tavia hissed. "When it comes to his safety, I'm not listening to anyone's demands. Bellmon's scared, and his decision-making is impaired."

"It doesn't matter. An entire police force is behind his decision. We're staying."

"You know he's wrong. I can see it on your face. I've seen it all night, every time you look at your girls. Look at them, and tell me they're safe."

"Keep your voice down," Dad growled.

Tavia leaned back, just enough to give Dad some space. She breathed out her nose. "We can sneak them out after dark."

"That's the worst time to travel."

"I live just past Main Street behind the grocery store," she said. Dad shook his head. "That's halfway across town."

"Well, where do you live?"

Dad looked at Halle and me and then down at Tobin. "Two-and-a-half blocks south." Tavia began to speak, but Dad interrupted, "One of those blocks is the park, so it's more like five or six."

"We can make it," Tavia said. "We can slip out right after dark and hide out at your place, like we're doing here, but it'd be safer—just until daylight."

"I don't even know you," Dad said. "Why should I listen to you?"

"Because I'm a parent with a little one in here—just like you. Bellmon isn't responsible for our children, Andrew. We are."

"There are more supplies here," Dad whispered.

I could see it in his eyes. He was considering it. I liked Tavia's idea, but I wouldn't dare say so. If a kid agreed, that would automatically make the plan weak.

"There are also more people. Think about the worst-case scenario. Do you wanna be in here, trying to get out, when that goes down? I sure as hell don't."

Dad looked around, thinking. He didn't take long in making up his mind. "We've got an hour before it's dark enough to try." His eyes fell on me. "We'll take turns watching the little ones while we each get supplies. I'll get medical. Tavia, you grab food. Jenna, you get water and two blankets just in case we don't make it to the house."

Tavia and I nodded.

Dad did, too. "I'm going to get back before anyone suspects anything. Act normal."

Tavia put her hand on my shoulder and sighed as Dad walked away. She closed her eyes and whispered a prayer. Then, she looked down at me. "Your dad's as smart as I thought he was."

"Most of the time."

He wasn't always worthy of father of the year, but I trusted him to get us to safety. He thought quickly, was handy with little to nothing, and had a decent aim. He'd even made me a console table once. When I was nine, I'd accidentally fallen on it, and it hadn't even wobbled. When he did things, he would do them right. Mom had even admitted once that she missed that about him. It seemed to be the only quality of his that she could appreciate. She could trust him to take care of things, and he would take care of us.

chapter five

"IT'S DARK," I said, rolling up a blanket and gesturing for Halle to hold it under her arm.

"So?" she said.

"I'm going to tell you a secret, and you have to be quiet about it. Okay?"

She gave a nod, already aware that she wasn't going to like what I had to say.

"Dad is going to take us home."

"But the governor—" she said.

I shushed her. "Tavia and Tobin are coming, too."

Halle's eyes bulged. "Is she the new girlfriend?"

"No. No, she's just a friend. They think it'll be safer if we go to Dad's house. Mom will go there, too, when she gets into town."

She frowned but agreed.

I leaned down to whisper in her ear, "You have to keep this a secret, Halle. We're going to sneak out. We're not supposed to leave."

"Will they shoot at us?" Halle asked. She was always one for theatrics, but she was genuinely afraid.

I shook my head, pretending to dismiss her concern. "No way, crazy pants."

Halle laughed once and rolled her eyes. When she turned, I swallowed hard.

What if the shots we heard were from those wannabe soldiers gunning people down who were wandering around? What if they shot Mom? I shook my head, pushing those thoughts from my mind.

More than one person had referred to my mom as a badass. No one would take her down before she got to us. By sheer will alone, she would find a way.

"This blanket is yours to hold," I said, holding out the tightly rolled wool.

"I don't want to hold it. You hold it," Halle whined.

"I'm holding the other one plus holding your hand."

She pressed her lips together.

"Halle, this is important. You have to hold this, and you can't draw attention to what we're doing."

She leaned toward me. "I have to go to the bathroom."

I sighed. "You just went."

"I'm nervous," she admitted.

I kissed her forehead. "Me, too. We'll go as soon as we get to Dad's. It's not far, I promise."

"But I have to go," Halle said again, desperation in her voice.

I looked to Dad. "We can't go yet," I whispered to him.

"What? Why?"

"Halle has to go to the restroom."

"Again?"

"She's nervous," I explained.

He sighed, frustrated. "Take her. Hurry. In and out."

I tugged on Halle's hand.

"The bathroom's that way," she said, resisting with every step.

"There's only one restroom, Halle, and there's a line. You're going to have to go outside."

"What? I'm not pottying outside!" she hissed.

I forced her out the door and to a dark corner of the yard. "Halle," I grunted. "Here. Squat."

"No!"

"We don't have time for this!" I said.

Our voices were no louder than a whisper. We were well practiced in fighting just loud enough so that no one could hear.

Halle grew sullen, her lips forming a hard line. "This. Is. Injustice," she said, unbuttoning her jeans.

"You don't even know what that means," I said, exasperated. I turned around but leaned back to murmur one last instruction out of the side of my mouth, "Don't go on your shoes."

"My pee feels hot. I think I'm running a fever."

"It's just cold outside. Hurry up."

"What if I'm infected?"

"You're not. Let's go."

Halle put herself together, and then I gestured to Dad that we were ready. Dad would go first in case anyone noticed, and then we would follow in twos.

Halle and I pretended to talk while Dad walked casually down the fence line, running his fingers along the chain links. To me, his nonchalance looked forced, but no one else seemed to notice. I kept Halle with me once Dad had slipped into the space between the two large gates. The young gunmen had closed the gates earlier with a rusted thick chain.

Dad was athletically built. He was on the department's softball team. He wasn't in the best shape of his life, but he easily maneuvered himself under the chain to the other side. Halle simply sidestepped through, but I had to duck. Dad kept walking toward the shadows of the trees, and Halle gripped my hand tighter.

A few moments later, I heard the chain rattle again.

Dad strolled across the street and into the park, and then he ducked behind a large tree trunk. When Halle and I reached him, he pulled us to the side.

"Wha—" I began, but Dad covered my mouth with his hand.

Halle's eyes danced between us. When Tavia made it to the tree with her son in her arms, Dad removed his hand from my mouth to hold his finger to his lips.

Tavia blinked.

"Can you keep him quiet?" Dad asked. He nearly breathed out the words.

Tavia raised an eyebrow.

"What if he's scared? Will he be quiet if you tell him to?"

"I am his mama. Nothing else is scarier than that," she whispered.

Dad tilted his head in the direction of the street on the other side of the armory. The police officers were mobilizing outside.

"Heads up!" one called.

"Halt!" another said.

"We're police officers! Halt, or we will fire!"

The commotion drew the attention of the groups of people in the yard. They walked over to the west fence. The yelling had also attracted the multitude of silhouettes wandering in the dark, their slow ambling only truly visible between streetlights. They were moving like children. Like bored grade-schoolers walking in a line to a field trip no one wanted to go on, they shuffled their feet in protest. Surely, they moved forward toward the officers without fear.

I'd watched enough movies with my mom to know what I was looking at. "They came from the highway, didn't they? They're infected," I said, not really asking.

"Last warning!" an officer commanded.

"Please stop!" another begged as he aimed and cocked his rifle.

The tornado sirens filled the air, an eerie rise and fall, echoing from each corner of town.

"Run," Tavia whispered.

I knew she was speaking to the people in the armory.

"Kids are in there, Dad. Little kids."

"Shh," he said.

"Kids Halle's age. Babies," I pleaded.

"We can't help them," he said.

Tavia picked up her son. "We should go. Before..." Her voice trailed off.

I was glad she hadn't said the words in front of Halle.

One of the police officers fired off a warning shot, but the river washed over him, his cries muffled, and then they moved on to the others.

"Go!" Dad took one stride and then stopped, yanking me back by the shirt. "Wait! Let's go around." He made a half circle in the air, pointing toward the east.

Tavia shook her head. "Let's just get there!"

Dad pulled on my shirt again, and I, in turn, pulled on Halle.

"Look," he said, gesturing to the road.

A few people from the yard had escaped despite the shooting, and they were running south down Sixth Street. It was just a handful at first, and then more appeared.

"C'mon, Tavia," I hissed as the screaming in the armory began.

"What's happening?" Halle cried.

I held my hand over her mouth as we walked quickly across the other street and down a small road with small houses. A dog began barking and rushed toward Dad, stopping only when its chain held him back. After a momentary pause, Dad encouraged us to continue.

We walked two blocks east and then turned south. The police were still shooting, but the shouting and screams had quieted down. Halle was whimpering but kept quiet. Tobin looked around with wide eyes and a finger in his mouth, but he hadn't made a peep.

Once we got to Dad's street, Dad held up his hand, and we froze. A man was bent over an animal that was collared and still attached to a chain. His head was bobbing up and down and then jerking from one side to the other as he yanked away the animal's flesh from the bone.

Dad held up his finger to his mouth, and he took a step back. I did the same, but Halle was behind me, and when she didn't move, I nearly tripped over her.

"Jenna!" she barked.

The man's head snapped up, and he crawled a couple of feet before fumbling himself up to his feet.

Dad swallowed. "Run," he said, his voice surprisingly even.

Tavia held on tight to Tobin as she turned on her heels and ran back the way we'd come. Dad brought up the rear, but Tavia began to fall behind. Dad ran back and took Tobin from her arms, and they ran together, puffing.

A light blinked once, catching our attention. Dad stopped and then pulled us across the street, up a few steps onto a porch, and straight through an open door.

In the dark living room stood an old man holding a small flashlight, sixtyish, with a short white beard and slits for eyes. Next to him was a much younger woman, maybe his daughter. She was plump and covered in freckles, her reddish-brown hair shaped like a Christmas tree.

"Thanks, Jerry," Dad said, trying to catch his breath. He handed Tobin to Tavia. "Sorry to hear about Marva."

I scanned the dusty frames on the walls. The same three people stood posed in all the photos. The only person in the pictures and not in the room with us was a woman with wavy silver hair, cut short and feathered back—Jerry's wife. I couldn't tell how long it had been since their last family photo. The redhead had the same hairstyle in every picture since she was around my age, and only Jerry's hair color had changed since then.

Halle crumpled against my side, trembling from the cold. I wrapped her in one of the blankets we carried from the armory and then my arms.

"Have you met the girls? That's Jenna"—Dad pointed to me— "and little Halle over there," he finished, lowering his finger toward Halle.

"I've seen 'em around town once in a while," Jerry said.

Dad looked at us and gestured to his friend. "Jerry is retired from the Navy. He's also a retired Anderson firefighter."

"Way before your time, Andy," Jerry said. "I'm an old fart. Never been gladder though. Heard they called all of you to the armory?"

Dad looked down. "We barely made it out."

"Who's Marva?" I asked.

Dad shifted, offering a quick apologetic smile to Jerry. "Marva is his wife."

"*Was* my wife," Jerry said. "We lost her to cancer last year. We sure miss her."

The house looked like it missed Marva, too. The living room had two worn couches and a dark green recliner, their backs turned to the kitchen. A counter covered in peeling Formica that looked older than Dad separated the two rooms.

Jerry continued, "This is my daughter, Cathy Lynn."

She gave a nod, smiling just enough not to seem rude. She had dark circles under her eyes. She didn't seem to like that we were there. She tugged on her Winnie the Pooh T-shirt. I thought her choice to wear a cartoon character was odd because she looked older than Dad.

Jerry gestured to his daughter. "I called her over when the news said the virus had hit Atlanta. I knew once it was on our soil, it would spread fast. She lives just down the road there. People just don't use common sense. Speaking of, what the hell were you doing out there, Andy?" Jerry asked, frowning. "Don't you know they're patrolling the streets? They're shooting people!"

"What?" Tavia asked.

Cathy Lynn pointed, her hands trembling. "On the corner. Greg Jarvis refused to go with them, and they shot him dead right in his front yard. Didn't you see him?"

Dad shook his head. "We were…preoccupied. The infection is in Anderson. We saw a man. He was…eating a dog, I think."

Jerry spit into the Styrofoam cup he was holding and nodded. "That was probably Greg. He's been walking around since about a minute after they put a bullet in his chest and drove away. Idiots. You gotta shoot 'em in the head, or they just get back up."

Dad and Tavia traded glances.

"One of the last reports on the news said that it spreads like rabies," Jerry said. "They bite ya, and if it don't kill you right away, you get sick enough to die. When you get up, you ain't you." He shook his head. "Just like in the movies. They were spot-on, goddamn it."

"Did they say anything else?" Tavia asked.

Jerry frowned. "Oh, they did mention the flu shots."

"What about them?" Dad asked, frowning.

"Did you get yours this year?"

Dad dipped his head once, the skin around his eyes tight. "Is that what's infecting people?"

"No," Jerry said. "Just the bite. But that blonde on channel nine said they heard several reports of people turning faster, once they're bit, if they had the flu shot. They don't know why. I've never liked her much—that reporter. She's probably safe. I hear zombies eat brains."

I chuckled, and Dad shot me a look.

"Did she say any more about the flu shot?" Tavia asked. "Did they ever say how much faster? Right after they've been bitten?" Tavia asked, turning her body to put a few inches more between her son and Dad.

"They didn't say," Jerry said.

Tavia's face switched from surprise to anger. "The government should have warned us. They should have told us the truth, so we could have been prepared."

Cathy Lynn raised an eyebrow. "Would you have believed them?"

Tavia patted and rubbed Tobin's back. He was already asleep, but she continued to gently bob and sway. "I knew when they started reporting on Germany this morning. If they had admitted it was the dead coming back to life, I damn well would have believed them, and I would have had more time to get supplies and protect my family."

Dad shook his head. "I wouldn't have. There's just no way. That's like admitting that vampires are real."

More gunshots popped, and they didn't sound far away.

"Kill that flashlight, Cathy!" Jerry hissed.

Cathy Lynn pressed the button. It was even darker than before, and Halle held on to me even tighter.

The moon poured in through the windows, highlighting just one side of Dad's face. He was looking around the room, his eyes dancing from the couch to the floor and past Jerry to the back of the house.

"Jerry, can we stay here until morning? I'm not sure it's safe to walk around at night. There are a lot more of those things. They're pouring in from the interstate. A hundred at least. Probably more."

"Sure, sure. Cathy will get you some blankets and pillows, won't you, Cathy?"

Cathy Lynn complied, turning toward wherever he kept his linens. She froze mid-step when another cluster of bullets cracked, even closer this time. "Dad, the closer the shooting gets, the closer those things get. We should board up the windows like the news lady said."

"I told you, we're not staying here. We're going to Bobby's farm at first light."

Cathy Lynn sighed. "But what about *tonight*?"

"She has a point," Tavia said.

I was scared before, but my panic was beginning to push the bile higher in my throat. The infection was no longer *over there*. It was right outside. It was waiting for us in the dark. I opened my mouth to tell Dad I was afraid, but then I looked down at Halle. She wasn't trembling from the cold. She was terrified. I'd barely noticed that she wasn't really talking. Usually, I couldn't get her to shut up. If I admitted to being afraid, she would lose it.

"We need to find Mom," I said.

"We will." Dad dipped his head once. Then, he turned to Jerry and Cathy Lynn to discuss fortifying the house for the night.

He wasn't thinking about how important it was to get to Mom, and it was making me beyond mad. She should be here by now.

What if she was one of the people on the interstate, trying to get on to the Anderson exit, when those idiots opened fire? What if she's hurt? What if she made it into town another way? She would look for us at Dad's house.

I pulled out my phone—no service. The battery was only at nineteen percent, and I didn't have my charger. I thought about how stupid it had been to check Facebook, Snapchat, and the news instead of charging my phone. The only thing that mattered was talking to Mom, and when I got service back, I wouldn't be able to call her.

"Do you have a charger for this?" I asked Jerry, holding up my smartphone.

He shook his head.

Cathy Lynn held out her hand. "I do."

I handed her my phone, and she took it.

"Dad," I said.

He half-turned before waving me away, and then he resumed his conversation.

"We can't stay here. We have to go to your house. Mom will look for us there."

"I want Mom!" Halle burst into tears.

"Jenna, for God's sake!" Dad knelt next to his youngest. "Halle, honey, you have to be quiet," he said, shushing her.

With her free arm, Tavia hugged me to her side. "I know you're anxious, baby girl. Don't you worry. We're going to find her."

I pointed to the door. "The house is a block and a half away!"

Dad grit his teeth. "Jenna—"

"She's there. I know it. She's a block or so away, and we're sitting here. If we don't get to your house, we'll miss her!"

"Jenna, quiet!" Dad growled.

My eyes filled with tears. "I'm going."

"Jenna!" Halle sobbed.

Dad grabbed me with one arm and Halle with the other, and he held us together in a tight hug. "Girls," he said, keeping his voice low and calm.

That surprised me. Usually, he made a bad situation worse.

"I know you're scared. I know you miss your mom. I know you want to be with her, and I will make sure that happens. But you've got to trust me. Can you do that? Please?"

I pressed my lips together, my bottom lip pulling up. Halle's sobs softened to snivels, and I resorted to crying frustrated but quiet tears into Dad's shoulder. Something deep inside told me that my mom was close and that she was feeling scared and desperate like I was. The urge to get to her was too strong to ignore, but I couldn't leave Halle, and she wouldn't leave without Dad.

"Okay?" Dad said. "First light."

I wiped my eyes and turned away from him. "Whatever."

chapter
SIX

THE EARLY MORNING SUN peeked through the plastic blinds hanging on the windows, highlighting the thousands of dust motes floating in the air.

Halle was curled up next to me, all but a tangled mess of blonde hair, covered in a thick woolen blanket. As the night had turned colder and the gunshots had fired closer, we'd held on to each other, and somewhere between the chill inside and the fear of what was outside, we'd fallen asleep.

I picked up my things and quickly stuffed them into Halle's backpack. Then, I nudged Tavia. Tobin had been fussy on and off all night. Tavia had said it was because he was in a new place and off his routine.

"Hey," Tavia said with a sleepy smile, propping her head with her arm. "We made it through the night."

Dad was already awake, standing by the door. "I haven't heard close shots since sunrise. Let's get moving."

He turned to see Jerry shuffling from his bedroom. The old man held out his hand, and Dad took it firmly.

"I can't thank you enough, Jerry."

"You sure you won't come with us? I've just got that Lincoln Town Car in the driveway, but we can make it work."

Dad shook his head. "My Tahoe is parked near the armory. Once we get our things, we'll head that way."

Jerry glanced at Tavia and a still-sleeping Tobin. "I hope it has three rows."

"It does," Dad said, smiling. He bent down next to Halle and gently prodded her awake.

She sat up, and Dad handed over her glasses. Looking around, she was confused at first, but then recognition lit her eyes, and they glossed over.

"Halle, we're okay," Dad said. "We're going home."

"Is Mom there?" she asked.

"We'll soon see," Tavia said with a wink.

Halle scrambled to her feet and joined me at the door. She lifted her glasses to wipe each of her eyes with the back of her hand.

I focused on the road to the east. It was hard to see against the bright sun, but I could tell the road was peppered with just four or five ambling people.

"Dad," I said.

He leaned toward the screen door.

Tavia lifted her son off the floor and into her arms before joining us at the door. "Seems like they move pretty slow. That guy from last night didn't catch up to us, even when he was chasin'."

Dad pressed on the metal lever before opening the door. "Give me Tobin. My house isn't quite two blocks away, and I don't see anything between here and there. Even if those things notice us, we can make it."

"We don't want them to notice us. Then, they'll follow us to the house," I said.

"True," Dad said, pausing to think. He looked to Halle. "No matter what, you can't scream. You can't make noise. We don't want to draw their attention. Do you understand?"

"I'll try," Halle said.

"Good girl." Dad kissed her forehead.

"Wait," I said before he walked out onto the porch. "What if something happens? What if we get separated?"

"We won't," he said.

"But what if we do?"

"Try to go the long way around. Try to keep anything from following you, but go to the house."

"Which one is yours?" Tavia asked.

"On the southwest corner of Fifth and McKinley. White house with a red porch. There's a detached garage in the back."

Tavia kissed her fingers and then touched Tobin's hand.

"Let's get moving," Dad said. "Jerry?" he called back. "Good luck."

Jerry and Cathy Lynn waved to us, and then we walked in a tight group down the sidewalk, heading west.

"Keep your eyes open for someone walking between these houses," Dad said.

Tobin was looking around. It was more because he was wondering what we were doing than trying to help. One of his fat hands had a fistful of Dad's shirt, and the other was in his mouth. "Mama," he said around his fingers.

"Hi, baby," Tavia whispered. "Be real quiet until we get there. Good boy."

The whole town was quiet, too quiet. No vehicles were driving down the street. No dogs were barking. No planes were overhead. The only sounds were the soles of our shoes padding along the sidewalk. It was very unsettling.

We crossed the intersection and then walked around to the back gate. It was open, and immediately, my heart began to pound against my rib cage.

"She's here!" I said before covering my mouth too late.

Dad handed Tobin off to his mother, and then he grabbed my sweatshirt. "Hold your horses." After pulling his keys from his pocket, he looked inside the large Plexiglas window that made up the top half of his back door. He sighed. "Someone broke the window."

"It was Mom!" I whispered, excited.

He turned around, his face pale. "Jenna, I know you're eager to see your Mom, but I'm going to look first. What if she's..." He trailed off, looking to Halle. "Just wait here until I get back."

Even though he hadn't finished, just him insinuating that Mom could have been bitten, turning into one of those things, made me feel sick to my stomach.

Dad turned the key and then the knob before pushing the door. It resisted, sticking like it always did, and then creaked as it opened. Any other time, that noise would barely register, but when the world was so quiet, any sound we made might as well be a dinner bell.

Dad walked onto the yellow-and-green linoleum kitchen floor. "Scarlet?" he called just barely loud enough for anyone to hear.

"Get ready to leave," Tavia said, glancing over her shoulder. "Just in case."

"I'm not leaving without my mom," I said.

"I have to potty," Halle said.

"Pee-pee," Tobin said.

Tavia patted his back. "Me, too."

Dad reappeared, all color gone from his face.

"Oh Lord Jesus," Tavia said. "She's not—"

"No," Dad said, rubbing his forehead with his thumb and index finger. "She's not here."

"What?" I shouldered past him. "Mom?" I called. "Mom!"

I searched each room in a panic. When I returned to the living room, Dad, Halle, Tobin, and Tavia were all staring at the wall.

The drips of black spray paint had dried a few inches below the words that Mom had hastily written on the wall.

"No!" I said, staring at the wall. "I told you! I told you she'd come here!"

Dad reached for me. I pushed him away, my shoes crunching on the glass piled on the carpet. She'd come here for us. She had just been a little over a block away, and we'd missed her.

Tavia put Tobin on the floor, but he was clinging to her leg, only one train in his hand.

"Jenna, you have to keep your voice down," Dad said.

Halle sniffed. "It's okay, Jenna. We'll just go to Red Hill. It's the safest place, remember? Mom said so."

I wiped my nose, looking to Dad. "We've got to get to your Tahoe. We can be there by this afternoon."

Dad shook his head. "Jenna, the interstate is blocked. You heard what that guy said."

I lowered my chin. "Mom made it here somehow. She knew she could get to Red Hill from here. We've got to leave now. She'll be worried sick if we wait too long."

"Jenna—" Dad began.

"I'm going!" I said. "I need her. I want to be with her"—tears streamed down my face—"for however long that might be. And if you won't go with me, I'll go by myself."

"No!" Halle threw her arms around me.

Tavia blinked and then looked to Dad. "What is Red Hill?"

Dad sighed. "It's a ranch, northwest of here and across the state line." He sighed. "I've never been there, Jenna. I don't know exactly where it's at."

"I do!" Halle took a breath and began to sing.

> *West on Highway 11*
> *On our way to heaven*
> *North on Highway 123.*
> *123? 123!*
> *Cross the border.*
> *That's an order!*
> *Left at the white tower.*
> *So Mom can clean the doctor's shower.*
> *Left at the cemetery.*
> *Creepy…and scary!*
> *First right!*
> *That's right!*
> *Red! Hill! Rooooooooad!*

Tavia smirked and put her hands on her hips. "Who knew? I've been traveling with Beyoncé all this time."

Halle beamed. It was the first time I'd seen her smile since Mom had dropped her off at school the morning before. That seemed like an entire lifetime ago.

"We know the way," I said to Dad. "You just have to drive us. It's secluded and stocked. Mom always said it would be the best place to go, and she's there."

He shook his head. "It's a long way, honey. We should wait here until things calm down."

I held up my hands and then let them fall to my thighs. "Dead people are walking around outside. We don't have time. She's waiting on us!"

"Okay!" Dad said. "Okay, just let me think."

"While you think," Tavia said, "we girls had better take advantage of a working bathroom. Let me take Tobin first."

Halle and I agreed, and then when they emerged, I led Halle in by the hand. In the dim room, she hummed from the toilet, and then she washed her hands as I sat down. I didn't realize until that moment just how much I'd needed to go.

"We have to be more careful," I said. "Don't want to get bladder infections."

"What do you mean?" Halle said.

"It's not good to hold it for so long," I said, walking over to the sink.

"Why would we need to hold it?"

"In case we don't get to the ranch today. If we have to take back roads and it takes a little longer, then we need to think about these things. We can't just go to the doctor, like we've done before."

Halle pretended to understand, but I knew she had no idea what was really going on. To her, it was scary, but she was on autopilot, just doing what she was told. At some point, it would finally set in that things would be different for a long time.

When we came out of the bathroom, Tobin was pushing his train on the floor.

"He's so good," I said.

Tavia crossed her arms, looking proud. "He always has been. Hardly cried as a baby. Everyone told me that he'd be a nightmare of a toddler, but you can see, he's my angel."

A shadow darkened the very spot where he played. A low moan mixed with a gurgling noise made us all freeze.

"Choo-choo!" Tobin said, shoving his train across the carpet.

His voice was soft, but the moaning grew louder. Tavia scooped him up off the floor and backed against the wall, motioning for him to be quiet. Together, Halle, Dad, and I slowly backed away from the window and went into the kitchen, joining Tavia and her son.

"Jenna, keep an eye on that window. Tavia, stay with Halle. I'm going to get supplies," Dad said.

"I'm going with you," I said. "I know what we need."

Dad frowned in confusion.

"Bottles of water, a can opener, flashlights, batteries, candles, socks. Mom and I watched those shows all the time. Let me help you."

"Watch the window," he commanded Tavia. He pointed to me and then the kitchen cabinets.

I went straight to the front closet and grabbed one of Dad's hunting backpacks, unzipped it, and then went into the kitchen, opening the silverware drawer. I packed three forks, two knives, and the can opener. Then, I opened the junk drawer and fished out the box of matches, a small bottle of hand sanitizer, a mini LED flashlight, two candlesticks, and a package of batteries. From the cabinets, I tossed in a package of beef jerky, some ramen noodles, sandwich bags, and ten cans of soup. I grimaced. They weighed down my pack quite a bit.

The bathroom was next, but my backpack was filling up fast. I grabbed the first-aid kit, rubbing alcohol, all the Tylenol and ibuprofen I could find, three washrags, insect repellent, two rolls of toilet paper, and sunscreen. I tried to find a small mirror but no such luck.

In the utility room, I opened the top cabinets where Dad kept all his hunting and camping gear. "Halle!" I called just above a whisper.

She crept in, looking up at me through her glasses. Her hair was still matted to her head.

"Empty your backpack."

"What? Why?" she said, already whining.

"Because we're going to need things to survive and not your nail polish. Empty it. Hurry."

"But we're going to Red Hill. We don't need a tarp."

"Halle!" I hissed.

She sighed as she let the straps fall off her shoulders, and then she pulled on the pink zipper. She turned it upside down, and a variety of useless junk fell to the floor.

I threw in a tightly rolled-up tarp, another flashlight, a canteen, a compass, and a full roll of duct tape.

"I can't find one of my backpacks or my 9mm," Dad said. He'd changed into one of his navy blue Anderson Fire Department T-shirts with matching cargo pants, and his standard-issue navy fleece pullover was tied around his waist. He still had on his heavy black boots laced up to the top. "They're gone, and so is the ammo."

My eyes brightened. "She took them."

Dad wasn't happy, but he didn't dwell on it for long.

"Do you have a leather jacket?" I asked.

"No. Why?" he asked.

I shrugged. "Zombies will bite right through that thing," I said, pointing to his pullover. "What else did you get?"

After he processed my words with an unsettled expression, he held up a long nylon bag, zipped closed. "My hunting rifle and plenty of ammo." He pointed to the rolled-up nylon on top of his pack. "The tent—just in case," he said to Halle. He tossed her a heavier coat. "I've got my good hunting knife and a multitool, and we still have those blankets from the armory."

"Halle, go get a few more bottles of water," I said. "Don't make your pack too heavy."

"I know." She turned on her heels.

I pushed air through my lips, and my cheeks bulged out. Her backpack already appeared to be weighing her down. She would be complaining about carrying it before too long.

I walked into Dad's bedroom and looked around before going into his closet. I took three sweatshirts, tying one around my waist, and three ball caps.

"No extra clothes?" he asked.

"We don't have the room." I looked at his nightstand and then back at him. Looking back at his nightstand, I lunged for it and pulled it open.

"What are you doing?" He tugged me back, like I knew he would.

But it was too late. The drawer was open, and there was an open box of condoms.

I snatched it up. "Bingo," I said, tossing it to him.

His eyes flitted everywhere but on me. He was clearly embarrassed and thoroughly confused.

"I got it from the survival show I watched with Mom. They have lots of uses. I'm not thinking ahead for you or anything. Gross." I looked back down to the open drawer and picked up a small sewing kit. "We might need this, too."

"Do we have everything?" he asked.

"No, but we don't have room for everything."

"Good job, kiddo."

I managed a smug grin. I'd been angry with him for so long that it felt weird to be nice.

Dad patted my shoulder. "We should get going if we're going to make it to Red Hill before dark. We don't know what's between here and there."

I followed him to the kitchen where Tavia stood, looking a bit more relaxed.

"All clear?" Dad asked.

"He walked on by." She swallowed. "I think it was the governor."

Dad rubbed the back of his neck. "Is there anything you need for Tobin before we go?"

"A couple of changes of clothes for both of us would be nice. Other than a few toys, child meds, a sippy cup, some wipes, and a bottle of lotion, he doesn't need much." She lifted him higher on her hip. "And I'd sure like to check to see if my brother made it to my house."

"Your brother?" Dad asked.

"He was on his way here. I thought he either didn't make it this far, or he got caught on the highway, but if Scarlet made it here, that gives me hope that Tobin did, too." When Dad gave her a look, she continued, "My son is named after my brother. He always made sure we were taken care of."

Dad bobbed his head once in understanding and then took in a deep breath. "All right. We'll walk back toward the armory. Stay together, keep your eyes out, and get to the Tahoe. We'll drive to Tavia's and grab their supplies, and then we'll head west."

"To Red Hill ranch," I said. "To Mom."

"Yes," Dad said, glancing at the paint on the wall. "I hope it's everything you say it is."

"It is," I said with confidence. "We just have to get there. The rest is easy."

Dad made a face. "You don't remember what it's like—your mom and I living under the same roof."

I rolled my eyes. "Things are different now. I don't think you're going to be spending too much time fighting about how much money she spent at Walmart."

Dad chuckled as he opened the back door, but then his smile faded. After a quick glance around, he waved at us to follow.

chapter seven

THE WALK TO THE ARMORY wasn't a straight shot. A few stragglers were left behind, shuffling slowly in the park. Dad guided us around them, and before I could even break a sweat, we were at his SUV.

The armory was still surrounded by vehicles. I wondered how many of those things walking aimlessly in the yard had never made it to their cars.

"Don't slam the door," I instructed Halle as I lifted her to the front passenger seat.

Her eyes were red and puffy, her golden hair matted to her head. I pondered if I looked as lost and terrified as she did.

Tavia climbed into the bench seat in the back with one arm, holding Tobin in the other. She settled him beside her, distracting him with his train long enough to stretch the lap belt across his waist. She patted his knee with that motherly it's-going-to-be-okay smile, and it made me miss Mom even more.

I climbed in after Tavia, sitting behind Halle in the captain's chair.

"Mama," Tobin said.

"Yes, baby?"

"I want cereal."

She nodded. "We're going home. I'll get you some while we're there." She smiled at him, but when she looked away, worry scrolled across her face. After today, she wasn't going to be able to provide him with food every time he asked for it.

"Can I take some of my toys?" he asked.

"Yes, but just a few. We'll have a lot more things you'll have to help Mama carry."

"Yes, Mama."

She kissed his forehead. "Good boy." She blinked her eyes and then looked up, trying to keep the tears from spilling over.

"Don't worry," I said. She looked to me. "You know what to do to keep him safe. Remember what you did at the armory. That was pretty brave."

Tavia's sweet smile peeked out from the corners of her mouth. "You think so?"

"What street do you live on?" Dad asked.

"Padon," Tavia said. "Behind the grocery store and across the street from the church."

"Got it," Dad said, continuing south. "That's right next door to Scarlet's grandparents' house."

"Richard and Helen are Scarlet's grandparents?" Tavia asked, surprised.

"Helen's my mema," Halle said, her cheery voice a strange contrast to the disturbing scene outside the SUV.

Tavia shook her head. "Small, small world."

"Even smaller now," I said, staring out the window.

It was a beautiful Saturday, but no kids were playing outside. Instead, there were monsters that weren't supposed to exist, bodies lying in the street, and the occasional crack of gunfire.

"Andrew?" Tavia said. "What if my brother is there? He's a big guy."

"Halle can sit behind me. He'll fit just fine in the passenger seat. There's plenty of room."

"Even with Richard and Helen?" she asked.

"We'll make it work," Dad said.

Tavia settled back into the seat and hummed a small laugh, resting her elbow on the door and her forehead in her hand. I'd never seen someone so full of relief.

Dad turned south onto Main Street, but he soon had to retreat to a side road because of the huge group of infected roaming in the street. A high-pitched ringing sound came from one of the businesses, but I couldn't figure out which one.

"It's weird how they're all on Main Street," I said.

"It's the security alarm at Gose Jewelers. They're attracted to sound." Dad slowed at the intersection, and even though the light was red, he didn't stop.

"No one else is on the road, Dad. Why are you slowing down?" I asked.

"Because you never know." His dad voice was making its debut for the day. "The first time I blow through an intersection, what will happen?"

Halle and I spoke in unison, both bored of the lesson already, "We'll get in a wreck."

"I see it all the time," Dad said as I mouthed his words at the exact same time.

Tavia snorted.

"What's so funny?" Dad asked.

"Nothing," Tavia answered, trying to keep from smiling.

Dad pulled to the side of the road and parked, leaving the SUV running. "Tavia," he warned, "try to keep your voice down."

"What?" Tavia said, looking up.

When she saw what Dad saw, she immediately covered Tobin's eyes. A man the size of an NFL player was lying in Tavia's front yard, his arms and legs sprawled out.

Tavia sucked in a few gasps of air and then looked down at Tobin with a firm look on her face. "Son, do not, under any circumstances, look out this window," she said, pointing to the glass. "Do you hear me?"

Tobin quickly bobbed his head.

She cupped his cheeks and kissed his forehead. "Good boy."

She pulled the handle and hopped out, and I followed her, again closing the door quietly. I froze when I saw two people standing over a lifeless body lying in the yard, holding hands.

"Mema!" I said, running to her.

She opened her arms. "Jenna!" She turned me away from the body. "Don't look, honey."

Mema was stick-thin, but she always gave the best hugs. She would hold me like she meant it, and she was never in a hurry to let go.

"Andrew!" Papa said when Dad stepped out of the Tahoe. "You've got both girls?"

"I do," Dad said.

"Have you seen Scarlet?" Mema asked, fussing with her short permed hair.

Dad slowly shook his head. "But she's okay." He looked over his shoulder, watching Tavia slowly approach.

She threw her arms out and let them slap her sides. She fell to her knees beside her brother with a lost look in her eyes. I had never witnessed that kind of devastation in a person—the kind that made me want to help, but I knew nothing would.

Tobin's clothes were full of holes, and he'd been shot a few times in the face. It was strange how the bullets had gone into his body smoothly and made such a mess on their way out. The front of Tavia's home was also pockmarked.

"Look away, Jenna," Dad said. "Tavia, I'm sorry."

Bent over her brother's body, she sobbed.

"But we have to go." He looked to my grandparents. "Get your things together. We're meeting Scarlet. We'll make room."

Papa put his arm around Mema. "Tell her we love her. We're staying put."

"Mema?" I said, looking up at her.

She squeezed me tight. "We're going to stay here at the house, sis."

Dad kneeled next to Tavia and put a gentle hand on her shoulder. "Tavia?"

"We can't just leave him here," she said, shrugging away from Dad's touch.

"We'll bury him," Papa said. "You have my word."

"Tobin," she cried, touching her cheek to his. "I'm sorry I wasn't here."

"Tavia, I hate to rush you, but we have to get going," Dad said.

She wiped her wet cheeks. Dad helped her to stand, and she took one more look at her brother before going inside her house.

Papa crossed his arms over his chest. "Poor guy. He never had a chance. See his ankle? Must have blown it out somehow on his way here. It's the size of a cantaloupe. Were you at the armory?"

"Yes. Were you?" Dad asked.

Papa shook his head. "Nope. No, those soldier wannabes picked us up. We didn't want to go, but the men said the governor ordered it. We were on our way when someone radioed that the armory was overrun. They let us out about four blocks from here. We walked the rest of the way. Wasn't easy though. We're not as spry as we used to be."

"It *was* overrun," I said. "It was awful."

Mema walked me back to the Tahoe and opened the passenger door to hug Halle. She had tears in her eyes.

"Give your mama kisses for me."

"What about Grandma?" I asked, meaning Mom's mom. "Have you heard from her?"

"Not yet," she said, her lip trembling. "Take care of each other."

She hugged us both, and I climbed into the backseat with Tobin.

The boy was kicking his feet back and forth, keeping his chin nearly to his chest, minding his mother exactly the way she'd asked.

"You okay, Tobin?"

"Yes." His eyes strained to look up at me. "It's my Uncle T, ain't it? Is he out there? I heard Mama crying."

I pressed my lips together. "Just...don't look outside. Your mom will be back soon."

"With cereal," he said, looking at his feet again.

Dad and Tavia entered the SUV a few moments later. Dad was holding a duffel bag, and Tavia had three plastic sacks and a bowl with a spoon.

"I just put a spot of milk in there, so it doesn't spill. We have to get on the road," she said. The whites of her eyes were red, the skin around them sagging, but she was trying to stay strong in front of her son. "Keep looking down until I say."

Tavia kept her eyes on her front lawn as Dad pulled away.

"Okay, baby. You can look around."

Tobin leaned his head against his mom, and she hugged him to her, holding her breath to keep from crying. She looked up at the ceiling and then straight forward. I could tell that she had decided to push it out of her mind for the moment.

We had a long road ahead, and we all had to stay focused. Besides not knowing the condition of the interstate overpass, we had four tiny towns to get through before Red Hill ranch.

"Daddy?" Halle said.

"Yes, honey?"

"I want Mom."

"I know," he said. "I'm trying."

chapter eight

"MERCIFUL JESUS," Tavia said.

Her mouth hung open as her eyes scanned the carnage on the interstate. Cars were facing in every direction, gridlocked so tightly that it looked like the hopeless last few seconds of a Tetris game.

Infected were ambling about—men, women, and children.

"Don't look, Halle!" I said, reaching up too late to cover her eyes.

"There are kids!" she said in a panic. "Why are they like that, Daddy? Why do they look like that? Are they dead?"

Dad drove slowly across the overpass, weaving between the various military vehicles and pickup trucks. Half-eaten men in camo were lying on the concrete, their weapons still in their hands.

Dad pressed the breaks gently until we came to a stop.

"What are you doing?" I said, afraid. "What are you doing, Dad?"

Before I could ask again, Dad was back inside the Tahoe with a huge rifle and a lot of ammo in his arms.

He set the gun, stock down, on the floorboard next to Halle. "Don't touch that," he said. "The safety's on, but until you learn how to shoot a gun, you don't need to handle one."

Halle quickly bobbed her head.

Dad switched the gear to Drive, and we continued forward.

Finally, we were at the edge of the overpass. A man, his suit tattered with bullet holes, reached out for the SUV, but we easily passed by him. He was wearing a wedding ring, and I wondered if his wife was wandering somewhere below, if he remembered her, or if they had any children. Maybe he had taken the interstate home, and his wife was waiting, looking out the window and thinking he'd pull into the driveway at any minute.

"Do you think they know they're alone?" I asked.

Tavia reached up to put her warm hand on my shoulder. "Who they were has left that body and gone on."

"To where?" Halle asked.

Tavia hesitated. "To a place where they can rest, where they aren't afraid, where they can't see this mess down here."

"I wanna go there," Halle said, absently twirling her hair, as she watched the pastures and farmhouses blur by.

Dad gave her a side glance. "Don't say that, honey." His voice was strained, and his Adam's apple bobbled as he swallowed down the sadness we all felt.

"Damn it," Dad grumbled.

"What is it?" Tavia asked.

"I meant to get gas when we got back into Anderson, but it slipped my mind."

"I can't imagine why," Tavia said. "Let's all keep an eye out for a gas station. Maybe we could stop at the next house and see if they have a gas can?"

"I can try to siphon off gas from a car, if I can find some tubing and a container," Dad said. "I've never done it before, so no promises."

"How low are we?" I asked.

"Don't ask," Dad said just as his dashboard chimed.

Tavia fidgeted and then asked anyway, "Did the gas light just come on?"

"Don't ask," Dad said again.

I clenched my teeth. *He knows what's happening, and he forgot to get gas?*

Tavia noticed the expression on my face and mouthed to me, *We're still okay.*

"Mama?" Tobin said.

"Yes, baby?"

"I wanna go home."

Tavia pulled her son's head against her side and kissed his temple. "Me, too, baby. Me, too."

Dad pulled into the long driveway of an old farmhouse sitting next to a much newer barn. The gravel crunched under the tires until the Tahoe came to a stop.

Dad turned off the engine. "Jenna, come with me. Tavia, I'm leaving the keys in the ignition. Stay with the kids."

I found that funny. Last week, Dad had told me that he didn't have to explain his decision not to take us to the theater—he wanted to hang out with Five and her son, who was much too young to sit through a cartoon, much less a movie—because I was a kid, and he was the adult. Now, when he talked about kids, he wasn't referring to me.

I shut the door most of the way and then pressed it closed. My black Converse made less noise against the gravel than Dad's boots, but it still sounded louder than it should have. I hopped onto the grass, and Dad took a wide sidestep to do the same. We smiled at each other and walked toward the house.

There were four steps to the side door, bordered in black iron rails. We climbed the steps together, and even that seemed too loud. There was no sound—no vehicles going by, no combines in the fields, no dogs barking, not even wind. I'd never realized how quiet the world could be without people in it.

Dad and I stood on the small concrete porch. The door was like Dad's—Plexiglas on top, wood on the bottom—except these people had a doggy door.

"Their dad got them a dog," I grumbled.

"Don't start," he said.

He tapped lightly on the Plexiglas.

"What good will that do?" I asked. "If any of those things are in there, that's not loud enough to draw them out. If people are inside, they won't hear us, and they will probably shoot us in the face if we—"

A man's face pressed against the door, and his mouth was open and wide, too wide. One of his cheeks had been chewed off. Dad and I startled. A smear of blood streaked across the window, and the man's molars were in full view.

"Don't look at it," Dad said.

"I don't want to, but I can't stop."

Another one, a woman, shouldered by the man and started clawing at the door.

"They can't open the door," Dad said.

I rolled my eyes. "Apocalypse level—genius."

"Okay, smart-ass. I'll be in the barn, being useful. Try to keep an eye on…them without looking too close."

I willed myself to look back at him, but I couldn't pull my line of sight away from the couple. The woman had a patch of hair missing from above her left ear, but that was the only wound I could see. Her skin was a bluish color, and her veins were a shade darker, visible underneath.

As they clumsily pawed at the door, I tried not to look into the vacant milky eyes of the woman. She wasn't overweight, but I couldn't help but notice her ill-fitting dress. Both of them had blood-covered chins and hands, and I found myself wondering who bit whom first.

Have they been feeding on one another?

Then, I saw it.

My chest heaved, and my eyes bulged. "Dad?" I took a step back. "Dad?" I called again, reaching for the railing.

I nearly fell off the top step. I stepped down backward and down again until I could no longer see it—the portable crib sitting against the wall in the living room behind the couple. The wall was spattered and smeared with blood, and the crib was saturated in it.

"Daddy!" I screamed.

He ran up behind me. "What? What is it?" he asked, breathing hard.

I buried my face into his torso, pointing with a trembling hand at the door. "They…they have a baby! It's—"

"In there?" Dad ran up the steps. After a few quiet moments, his footsteps could be heard on the steps, and then he pulled me against him again. "Christ almighty, Jenna. Think about something else. Think about your mom. Think about school. Anything else."

I shook my head, wiping my wet face on his T-shirt, while he comforted me. "They—"

He held my chin in his hand and lifted it. "No, they didn't. Remember what Tavia said—about how they're not the same as they were before?"

"The baby didn't know that."

Dad clenched his jaw and then turned toward the SUV. "C'mon, let's get out of here. There's a station down the road."

"Can we make it?"

"Yeah. I just didn't want to chance it. Jenna?"

"Yeah?"

"Don't tell Halle. Don't tell any of them. Let's pretend that we didn't see it."

I nodded, wiping my eyes.

"Any luck?" Tavia asked when we got back into the vehicle.

Halle and Tobin were coloring.

Dad shook his head.

Tavia's eyebrows pulled together. "Jenna? You all right, honey?"

"I'll be okay."

"Andrew, what's wrong with her?"

"Nothing."

Halle turned around in her seat, her elbows perched on the console. "What did you see?"

Dad turned, too. "Don't answer, Jenna." He looked to Tavia. "You don't want to know. Some things you can't unsee."

Tavia covered her mouth as Dad backed out of the driveway, and then she reached up to grab my hand, squeezing tightly. We both knew that was just one of the first of many awful things I would see, that we would all see. Even when we wanted to look away, we would have to stare ugly things in the face just to stay alive.

Halle turned around, and I closed my eyes. It was only a matter of time before she would have that last bit of innocence taken from her, too. I couldn't cover her eyes forever.

Dad pulled out onto the road, turning west.

West on Highway 11.
On our way to heaven...
Right after we get through hell.

The gas station was in the next town, but no one was manning the store inside. Dad used his credit card, whispering prayers I couldn't quite make out. Then, he punched the air, the vein in his forehead bulging. He crossed his arms on the back corner of the Tahoe and rested his head.

"What's wrong?" I asked.

"I think something has to be tripped in there. I hope," he said, narrowing his eyes at the store.

It was smaller than small. Dad reached inside, his feet coming off the ground, as he leaned over his seat toward the passenger side and grabbed his rifle.

"What are you doing?"

He cocked the gun. "I'm going to see if I can get the juice flowing. Can you try to run the card out here? Just do this." He showed me how to insert the card into the slit and then pull it out. "Choose the grade by pressing the eighty-seven button," he instructed, pressing it. "Then, take the pump off the holder and pull up the lever. The nozzle fits into the gas tank, like this, and squeeze the trigger," he said as I watched him act it all out. "You got it?"

"I can do it."

Tavia leaned out of her open window. "You didn't have to go through all that. I can do it."

"She needs to learn. She needs to learn everything," Dad said, keeping his eyes on the store. He held the rifle in front of him with both hands and took his first step.

"Be careful," I said. "They can sneak up on you."

Dad didn't turn around. When he reached the double doors, he banged on the glass with the stock of his gun. After nothing happened, he went inside.

I dipped the card into the slot, chose the grade, and then lifted the nozzle before placing it into the mouth of the SUV's tank. The gas pump beeped again, but again, nothing happened, and the digital display returned to scrolling words.

Dad popped his head out of the door. "Try it one more time. I think I figured it out."

I ran the card, but this time it was denied. "What? No," I said, trying it again. The word *Denied* came up again.

Dad pushed through the doors and held up his hands, frustrated and confused.

"It says the card is denied!" I yelled.

He jogged over to me.

"She's right," Tavia said. "I was watching."

"Damn it. Damn it!" Dad yelled to the sky. He pushed his palms against the driver's side door, his fingertips turning white, his jaw muscles working beneath the skin. "We have to go back to Anderson."

"What? No. We'll go as far as we can, and then we'll walk the rest of the way," I said.

Dad glared at me. "With a toddler and a seven-year-old? Jenna, that's not realistic."

"We have a tent. We have everything we need. We'll keep watch. We can find an empty house. We can make it."

"It's too dangerous. Those things are everywhere! We're going back."

"Mom isn't in Anderson."

"Jenna, something bad could happen. Are you willing to risk your sister's life? Your mom wouldn't want that."

"She didn't stay in Anderson because she knew we couldn't survive there. We've talked about it. We—"

"I said no," Dad said, his tone final.

"You weren't there! You don't get to make this decision! This is something Halle and I promised to Mom!"

"If she were that worried about riding this out with you, she wouldn't have left. She was right there, Jenna, and she left!"

"Andrew!" Tavia scolded.

Tears filled my eyes and spilled down my cheeks.

Dad's shoulders fell. "Damn it. Jenna, I'm sorry. I didn't mean it. I'm just frustrated."

"She didn't leave us. She is meeting us at Red Hill. That's the plan. It's always been the plan," I said, sniffing.

"You're right," Dad said, his cheeks flushed.

"She didn't leave us," I said again, mostly to myself. "I know her. I know exactly what she is thinking. I would have done the same thing! She wasn't sure if we would come back to your house. She knew where we would go though because we promised each other, and we keep our promises."

Dad bobbed his head. "Load up. Let's go."

I climbed into the back, next to Tobin, crossing my arms, and Dad sat in the driver's seat. He turned the ignition. The engine started, then sputtered, and died.

"No…c'mon…" He turned it again.

The engine made a whirring sound, but it didn't catch this time. Dad slapped the steering wheel with both hands.

"Andrew," Tavia said, her voice low and soothing, "we can walk. We can make it. It'll just take us longer than originally planned."

Dad nodded and ruffled Halle's matted hair. "Okay, Pop Can, get your backpack. Take as much as you can carry."

Halle obeyed, pulling her backpack over her shoulders.

chapter nine

WE KEPT TO THE ROAD.

Dad half-hoped a car would pass us and pull over, but he also worried that someone would try to take our stuff. I didn't tell him that it was unlikely since it was only day two, and most people were either worried about getting home to their loved ones or concentrating on fortifying where they were.

"You don't know that, Jenna. Everything you know is based on television shows," Dad scolded.

"Which are based on common sense and historical facts," I said.

"There has never been a zombie outbreak before."

"But there've been disasters before. The behavior is the same."

Dad sighed and shook his head. Then, he stopped and turned around. "Want me to carry him?"

Tobin had fallen asleep half an hour before, and Tavia had fallen further behind the longer we walked. She shook her head, too tired to talk.

Dad double-backed toward her, his arms out in front of him. "Give him to me. You're no use if you're exhausted. We still have fourteen miles to make before dark."

Tavia's chest heaved, handing her son over. "I'm really regretting my excuses not to walk with my friend Teresa."

Dad chuckled, but his smile vanished when Halle pointed.

"Daddy!" she said, alarmed.

One of those things, a man, was stumbling toward us.

"It's alone," Dad said. "Probably from the next town. We'll make a wide run around him and then run for a while to stay ahead of him."

"I can't run," Tavia said, breathless.

The thing was coming closer.

Dad looked around. "We could find a place to hide, but he'll probably just follow. Either way, we'll have to pick up the pace."

"If we kill it, we don't have to," I said.

Everyone looked at me.

"I'll run around with Halle. You distract it. When he turns around, kick his knees out from under him, and then hit him in the head with the butt of your rifle."

Dad's eyebrows shot up.

I shrugged. "Or we can run."

"What kind of stuff was your mom letting you watch?" he asked.

"That was from a video game. Are we going to run or not?" I asked.

Dad and Tavia looked at each other.

"I'm sorry, Andrew. I just can't."

Dad breathed out as he handed Tobin to Tavia. Dad rubbed the back of his neck and then pulled the strap of his rifle over his head. "Yesterday, I never would have believed that I'd be bashing someone's head in."

"I didn't think I'd be bait either. We all have jobs to do."

He glared at me. "Don't watch—either of you. I don't want you to see me doing this."

"Just make sure you kick out his knees," I said. "It'll be a lot easier."

I knelt down, and Halle climbed onto my back. I jerked up, adjusting her position.

"In theory," Dad said. "Go on. Give yourself plenty of room."

We walked another twenty seconds. Then, Tavia stopped, Dad readied himself, and I ran to the right in a wide half circle. The man moaned, reaching for us.

"Hey!" I said. "This way!"

He turned to follow, his bloody Oklahoma Sooners shirt ripped at the collar. Raw meat and bone were visible, but the blood wasn't fresh. Something had chewed on him but not for long.

I heard Dad grunt, and I turned, but I didn't come to a full stop. The infected fell just like I'd said it would, but when Dad hit its head with the stock of his rifle, it kept reaching for him.

"Hit it again!" I yelled.

Dad swung again, and a loud crack echoed in every direction. It was finally still. Dad nudged it with his boot and then stomped over to Halle and me.

"I thought I told you not to watch!" he growled.

I looked back and up at Halle whose hand was over her glasses. "She didn't."

"You! I told you, too!"

"I can't keep my eyes closed, Dad! I have to see what's coming!"

He thought about that for a moment, still breathing hard. Different emotions scrolled across his face, and then he bobbed his head once before wiping the remnants of the infected's brain matter off his gun and onto the grass.

"Good job," Tavia said when she caught up to us.

Dad took Tobin again, and we continued on, almost as if nothing had happened.

I kept Halle on my back, knowing we still had a long way to go. She silently thanked me by touching her cheek to the crown of my head and giving me the slightest squeeze. I grinned. For us, getting along was a rarity. When I wasn't antagonizing her, she would be bossing me around. We had become so accustomed to fighting that we'd often yell at each other for no reason at all.

But now, the world had shifted, and so had the things I cared about. The most important thing to me was Halle, and even after two miles with her small yet surprisingly heavy frame, the goal of getting her to Mom kept my feet moving forward.

We talked while we walked. We ate while we walked. We drank and laughed. All the while, we moved toward the next town, only pausing for bathroom breaks.

"I'm hungry," Halle said just as we reached the crest of a hill.

The sun was hot, and none of us were used to hiking such a distance.

"It's snack time, isn't it?" she asked.

"We've got to conserve food, Halle. We don't know how long we'll be out here."

"What does that mean?" Halle asked.

I held out my hand to her. "It means, we can't have snacks. Three meals a day—that's it until we find more food."

Halle frowned. "But we'll be with Mom tonight. She can make us something for dinner."

"We won't see Mom tonight unless we find a car. It's a long way on foot."

"How long?" she asked.

Dad glanced back at me. When I didn't have an answer, his expression perked up. "Maybe a couple of days, Pop Can. No worries. We'll get there."

"A couple of days?" she asked, her tone rising with each word.

I cringed. Dad did, too.

"Sorry, kiddo." That was all he could offer.

I squeezed her hand. "The more we walk, the closer we get."

"No snacks?" she whined, her bottom lip pulling up.

At the top of the next hill, for only the third time in as many hours, we stopped.

Tobin pointed. "What's that?"

"Jesus in Heaven," Tavia said, dabbing the sweat from her neck and chest.

"Infected," Dad said. "Maybe ten?"

Tavia held her fingers to her forehead to block out the sun. "They're too far away. Maybe they're people?"

Dad pulled his binoculars from his bag and held them up to his eyes. He quickly pulled them back down. "Damn it."

"What do we do?" Tavia asked.

"We can't get through them," Dad said. "All there is between us and them is pasture."

I looked around. "See any farmhouses or barns?"

Dad used his binoculars and turned in every direction. "Just a pump house. Doesn't look big enough for all of us to fit."

"Okay," Tavia said. "What do we do?"

Dad held out his hands and then let them hit his thighs. "Find a place to hide? Hope they turn in a different direction?"

"You've got a scope," I said. "Use it."

Dad looked down at his gun. "You just want me to open fire on a bunch of pe—"

"Infected, Dad. You said it yourself. They're infected. And there are too many of them to handle."

Dad's T-shirt was damp with sweat. Still, he used it to wipe his face. His five o'clock shadow was crowding his dry lips.

"Dad?" I said.

"I'm thinking."

"You've also got the gun you took off the bridge."

"I know." He narrowed his eyes at a row of round hay bales. "Tavia, get the kids on top of those. I'll climb onto one a little closer and then fall back to you if I have to."

"That's your plan?" I asked.

Dad grit his teeth. "Jenna, damn it, would you just do what I say?"

"I know how to shoot a rifle," I said.

"No."

"But—"

"I said, no! Now, get your ass on that hay!" He pointed with one hand and thrust the binoculars at me with the other.

I frowned as I snatched the binoculars from his hand, and then I led Halle to the field, stepping through freshly cut grass to the round bales.

Gripping his hunting rifle, and with the semiautomatic hanging from his shoulder strap, Dad walked west, toward the group of infected. I helped Halle climb up first, and she helped pull Tobin while Tavia and I pushed. Then, I cupped my hands and helped give Tavia a leg up. It wasn't perfect, and it took her a couple of tries, but she finally climbed to the top and then reached down for me.

"I've got it," I said.

"You sure, honey?" She watched me climb to the top.

"Yep," I said, breathless but smiling, as I sat next to her.

My mood didn't last long. I held the binoculars up to my eyes and located my dad. "He's picking a round bale. They're still a ways from him."

"It's *stucky*," Tobin said, trying to wipe the hay off his hands.

"It's just for a bit," Tavia said, pulling him onto her lap and brushing the hay from his clothes.

"He's getting into position." I watched Dad lay onto his stomach before he pulled the pin on his rifle. "I hope he remembered to keep his ammo handy."

Tavia hummed in disapproval. "You sure don't trust your dad, do ya?"

I lowered the binoculars and looked at her. "He...yeah, he's smart. But my mom loves this stuff. I just wish she were here. She thinks ahead. Dad thinks about...girls."

"I bet she doesn't love it now, and I bet the only girls your dad is thinking about are his own."

I made a face, embarrassed, and then I put the binoculars back up to my eyes just as Dad took the first shot. "He got one!"

He shot again, and his body jerked with the recoil.

"He got another one!" I let the binoculars fall to my lap. "It's really loud. It's going to draw more."

"We'll just have to skedaddle before then, won't we?" Tavia said.

Dad shot several more times. He didn't even have to fall back. He took down most of them and then hollered at us to climb down.

"C'mon, Halle!" I said after I hopped down. "Jump!"

She leaned over, her hands reaching out for me, and then she fell forward. I barely caught her. I set her feet on the ground and then held out my hands while Tavia lowered Tobin to me.

"Hurry!" I said to Tavia.

She climbed down fairly quickly, and we jogged to the hay bale Dad had shot from, but he was on the other side of the road, diverting the few infected that he couldn't bring himself to shoot.

"Look away, Halle," I said.

Tavia shielded Tobin's eyes as we hurried past, a tiny sob escaping from her throat.

Dad danced around the infected children with various wounds, all three of them younger than me. I only looked long enough to make sure they weren't following. When I heard three cracks, my shoulders shot up to my ears.

"Did you…" I began.

Dad shook his head, having a hard time with concealing his emotions. "Just made sure they couldn't keep up. Walk faster."

He picked up the pace, and we did the same, desperately wanting to create distance between us and the mess of bodies we'd left behind.

In the distance was a field full of scrap metal, old cars, and a few rusted tractors.

"Daddy! Cars!" Halle said.

"We won't be going anywhere in any of those, Pop Can. They're just there for parts."

"Oh," she said, deflated.

"Cars, Mama!" Tobin said, pointing.

Tavia touched her fingers to his dark hair. "That's right! You are so smart!"

He hugged his train.

If we had to travel with a toddler, I'd pick Tobin any day. He was quiet, and he minded his mother. Tavia could keep him calm when necessary. We had been so lucky so far. I wondered how long that would hold out.

"Cars, Mama!" Tobin said again.

An engine sounded in the distance, and Dad herded us off the road. The sun hit the vehicle just right, so it took a minute for me to see that it was a silver minivan. They were going so fast that I wondered if someone was chasing them, but the moment they saw us, the tires slowed.

A man about Dad's age rolled down the window. A dark beard surrounded his hesitant but polite smile. "Going to the next town?"

His wife sat in the passenger seat, looking behind her and whispering, comforting whoever was in the backseat.

"For now," Dad said. "We ran out of gas a ways back."

The man looked to his wife, and she gave her permission.

"Listen," he said, looking to Dad, "it's too dangerous to walk. We're headed to Shallot. My in-laws live there. We've been driving all night from Midland."

"You made it here all the way from Midland?" Dad asked.

"It wasn't easy," the man said, holding up a pistol.

His wife held up one, too, looking sheepish.

Dad glanced down the road. "We would appreciate you taking us as far as you can. I have some money—"

The man held up his hand and shook his head. "It'll be a tight fit with the kids back there, but you're welcome to ride along."

Dad turned to Tavia, and she let out a breath of relief.

"Thank you, Jesus," she said. "C'mon, Tobin. You found us a car!"

The man hit a button on the ceiling, and the side door slid open, revealing a girl a little older than Halle, maybe ten or eleven, and a boy Tobin's age.

"Well, hello there!" Tavia made her way to the third row, past the two captain's chairs the children were seated in.

She sat next to the wall and situated Tobin on her lap, leaving plenty of room for Halle and me, but I wondered where Dad would fit.

"Just, uh…your littlest can fit nicely on the floor between our kids, if you don't mind," the man said.

Dad climbed in and sat near the other wall, and I sat in the middle. Halle sat on the floor in front of my feet, scooting back against my legs.

The door glided closed, and then the man pressed on the gas. A wave of relief washed over me.

"I'm Brad," he said, looking into the rearview mirror for a moment. "My wife, Darla," he said.

She turned around and flashed a sweet smile.

"Our daughter is Madelyn, and our son is Logan."

Dad pointed to himself. "Andrew." He pointed to the rest of us. "Tavia, Tobin, Jenna. And Halle is on the floor."

Everyone traded the customary nice-to-meet-yous.

For the first time in hours, I felt my body slowly relaxing from being on alert since I'd opened my eyes that morning. It didn't take long to realize that none of us smelled very good.

"Dad," I whispered, "we are stinking up their car."

"Sorry," Dad said to the adults in front. "We've been walking all day. We don't mean to offend."

"Don't worry about it. We're not at our best either," Brad said. "Her parents were supposed to head down to visit later today, but when we heard the reports, we knew they wouldn't chance it, and Shallot is tiny. We'll have a better chance there than in Midland. Her parents would worry if we didn't come."

"I'm taking the girls to their mom. She's not far from there."

"If we can, maybe we could run you up there in the morning? Depending on the gas situation, of course. We just used our last can an hour ago."

"That would be…" Dad laughed once, his shoulders relaxing as relief washed over him. "That would be extremely kind of you." He hooked his arm around my neck and pulled my temple to his lips. "We're going to be okay, kiddo. You'll be with your mom this time tomorrow."

"Don't jinx it," I said. "We're not there yet."

chapter ten

"WHAT THE HELL?" Brad said, stomping on the brakes.

Just as I reached for and missed Halle, Darla whipped around and caught her before she hit face-first into the console.

"Whoa!" Darla smiled at Halle when she looked up. "You okay, sweetie?"

Halle nodded, and then Darla looked expectantly at her own kids. They bobbed their heads at the same time.

Dad leaned forward. "What is it?"

Brad was watching the north side of the road, and we all—with hesitation—moved our lines of sight in the same direction.

An old two-story church was crawling with those things, as if it had been infected itself. They wriggled in and out of the broken stained-glass windows, like maggots squirming in the open wounds of a dead animal. Large shards of partial picturesque art hung from the tops of the window panes, and the jagged edges of wooden planks stuck out from the walls from which they were still nailed.

"Do you think people are stuck in there?" I asked.

"Lord, I hope not," Tavia said, her big eyes looking up toward the second floor.

Brad drove past slowly, and he pointed up. "Look there! An open window! They got out!"

"But look at all the blood on the side of the building," I said, noting the dark red smear leading from the AC unit to the roof.

"Mommy?" Madelyn said, her voice trembling.

"It's okay, honey. We're going."

The infected noticed the van, and one by one, they began filtering out of the church.

"Go, Brad," Darla warned. "Hurry!"

Brad pressed on the gas, and the van surged forward. Just as he got back up to speed, someone ran in front of the van, a woman, with her hands waving in the air.

"Stop!" she screamed. "Please!"

"Brad!" Darla shrieked.

Brad yanked the wheel to the right, crashing hard into a truck parked in the middle of the road. I managed to grab Halle this time, holding her shirt tight in my fists. She flew forward, toward the driver's seat, and my shoulder rammed into Logan's booster seat, but I didn't let go. The shirt choked Halle for half a second, but other than that, she was unharmed.

Tobin was crying, and Tavia was checking him over.

Brad and Darla both looked dazed, half-wondering what had happened and half-worrying what would happen next.

"Mommy!" Madelyn said again.

Logan began crying, too.

"Andrew! Is Tobin okay? He hit his head!" Tavia said with a strained voice. She was trying to keep calm.

Dad reached for him and pulled down one of his lower lids to get a good look in his eye.

"We've got to get out of here," Brad said. "Unbuckle your seat belt, Maddy!"

"Open the door!" I said, lunging forward.

Madelyn reached for me, so I helped her get unbuckled, and then I did the same with Logan. I put my hands under Halle's arms and lifted her up and forward, taking a big step out of the passenger's side sliding door. I was glad this van was the kind that opened on both sides. We wouldn't have been able to get out on the other side.

I glanced back at the church, at least a quarter of a mile behind us. "Halle?" I said, leaning down to look into her eyes. "Are you okay?"

"My throat hurts," she said, rubbing the red line the collar of her shirt had left.

"Sorry," I said, hugging her.

I took a quick sweep around the truck and van, looking for any more infected, and then I stopped at the front. The two vehicles, an old green truck and Brad's silver van, were twisted together, both of their guts exposed and intertwined.

An oozing dark liquid crept slowly from beneath the wreckage. "Something is leaking!" I said, pushing Halle backward.

Dad appeared next to me, holding Tobin. "That's...not from the van. That's..."

I leaned down to peek under the mangled vehicles to see a waif of a girl, not much older than me, lying beneath the van. One of her arms had been severed by the driver's side tire, and it was barely visible behind the tire.

"Oh my God, did I hit someone?" Brad said.

Darla covered her mouth.

"She was already dead," I said. "She was shot in the head. Probably infected."

Dad leaned down. "Looks like she'd been sick a long time before catching the zombie virus."

"Don't say that," Darla said. "Zombies—that's ridiculous," she spoke the words with a nervous giggle, like it was against her nature to speak up like that, but she had to say it out loud just for her own sanity.

"Are you okay?"

We all turned around to see a woman standing in a dress. It was once a red dress with white polka dots. Now, it was just red. One section of her frazzled dark hair was still tied back. Three children, a girl and two boys, stood behind her, wide-eyed and afraid.

"Are you all right?" she asked.

"Are we all right?" Brad stepped toward her, his expression severe.

She retreated back a step, holding her arms out, shielding the children with her body.

"We had a perfectly good vehicle! We were nearly to our destination! What the hell were you thinking, running out in the road like that?"

"I'm sorry," she said, her eyes glistening. "I was trying to get us a ride out of here."

"Brad," Darla said, touching his arm.

Brad pulled away from his wife. "A ride? How did that work out for you? Now, none of us have a damn ride! I have kids, too! You nearly got them killed!"

"I was...I was desperate!" she said, taking a step forward. "The town is overrun. It's just me and these kids, and I...I wasn't thinking. I'm so sorry."

Brad looked back at the vehicle and then threw his keys. They skipped across the asphalt and landed somewhere in the grass on the other side.

"Can...can we start over?" she asked. "My name is April. I have a house over there. You're welcome to stay. Please...please stay."

"Get your bags," Dad said. "We have to move."

"We have a house," the woman said. "O-over there. My husband boarded up some of the windows. If we're quiet, they won't bother us."

"Where's he?" Dad asked.

Her eyes danced between each of us, and then she simply shook her head.

The little girl—her hair, when it was clean, was probably nearly white—was younger than Tobin and Logan but not by much. She reminded me a lot of Halle when she had been that age. The boys were younger than me and looked nothing alike. They were scared to death. The older one had big green eyes and a splash of freckles across his nose, and the younger one had brown eyes, his sandy-blond hair already overdue for a haircut.

Tavia glanced at the approaching mob of infected slowly limping and stumbling toward us from the church.

"We'll have to run," the woman said. "We can lose them around the elementary school, and then we can sneak in through the back."

"Of the school?" Darla asked.

She shook her head. "It's full. You don't wanna go in there. Not all the kids were picked up in time, and..." She trailed off, blinking away whatever images were in her head.

"C'mon, boys," she said after picking up the little girl.

We quickly gathered our belongings and followed. We ran into the grass on the south side of the road, went across an overgrown empty lot, and continued behind the elementary school. The woman stopped there, her labored breathing making her chest heave. Dad was holding Tobin for Tavia, and Brad was carrying Logan.

We had way too many little kids in our party. No one who got far on zombie television shows ever had this many kids under ten.

Once we were all standing behind the tin exterior wall of the school, the woman took off again. We made a half circle and then snuck into a backyard through a gate. She gestured for us to go inside and then put her finger against her lips. After we did so, she quietly shut the gate behind her.

We stood in what looked like a former single-car garage that had been turned into a bedroom. A set of French doors led into the rest of the house. Dad handed Tavia's son to her, and then he turned the knob of the door on the right, slow and cautious. He was holding his rifle with both hands. Brad and Darla held their kids close, and Tavia moved to the side while the woman joined us. She closed the back door softly and turned the lock.

"What is he doing?" she whispered.

All three of her kids were standing against the wall, eyeing us warily.

"Checking to see if anyone else is in here," Brad said, keeping his voice low.

"No one is here," she said, shaking her head. "Just me and the kids."

"We need to make sure," Brad said.

Gunshots could be heard, popping like firecrackers somewhere nearby. It reminded me of the Fourth of July, but it definitely didn't feel like it.

Dad appeared in the doorway. "It's just us," he whispered.

He turned on his heels, and we followed him down a hallway that opened into a kitchen. The lights were off, and it would have been dark but for one broken window. Jagged edges of plywood hung from the nails driven into the wall.

Dad gestured to the unsecured window. "We need to patch that up—now."

"There are more sheets of plywood in the garage outside. We should have enough to double up on most if you'd like."

Dad complied, following her outside. They returned less than ten minutes later. April was carrying a toolbox, and Dad was grunting and walking awkwardly with the stack of plywood sheets in both hands.

Once Brad and my dad were finished refortifying the windows, only the few holes in the wooden sheets offered enough sunshine to see. I'd worried about the noise from the hammering, but Tavia had kept an eye out, and she'd said any curious infected kept being drawn the other direction, toward the sound of the gunshots. They were now just popping off one at a time. It was more sporadic, but they were still happening.

I made my way to the table and pulled out a chair. My leg muscles were still burning from our long walk.

Dad and Tavia immediately got to work with making us a small meal. Brad and Darla did the same for Madelyn and Logan.

The woman and her children just watched.

Darla's eyebrows pulled in. "Haven't you got any food?"

"We've already eaten. You go ahead," she said.

"We haven't got much left, but you're welcome to share," Darla said.

The woman walked with pride over to a door. She opened it to reveal a deep pantry with a decent stock of various cans of vegetables, rice, bread, peanut butter, chips, cereal, boxed stuffing, and bottles of water, and that was just what I could see right away.

"You're welcome to ours, too," she said.

"Goodness me," Tavia said, holding her palm to her chest.

Dad frowned. "You had all this food, yet you were so desperate to leave that you nearly got yourself mowed down in front of your kids?"

I raised an eyebrow. I was fairly impressed with him at that moment.

The woman looked at her kids and then back at Dad. "I'm scared. I was over there at that church when it was overrun, and we lost a lot of friends."

"So has everyone else." Dad scoffed.

"I lost my husband." A gunshot outside served as the period to her sentence.

Dad didn't have a response to that.

"I'm alone with these kids. I saw your van, and I panicked. I didn't know if we were leaving or you were staying. I just knew I couldn't keep us all alive by myself."

Tavia touched her arm. "You're not by yourself anymore. I'm Tavia. That's my son, Tobin," she said, pointing.

"My daughter's name is Nora, and my son is Jud."

"And who's this?" Darla was referring to the boy who looked to be around seven or eight, gauging by his oversized front teeth and his baby teeth on the bottom.

The boy spoke up, "Did you see that blood streak on the side of the church?"

Some of us nodded.

"That was from my teacher, Miss Stephens. She saved me from my parents when they were trying to kill me," he said the words matter-of-factly, as if he were talking about something that had happened at school that day.

Darla gasped, and Tavia's hand flew up to her mouth. Halle looked to me, not knowing how to react. Since it had all began, all I could think about was getting to my mom. I hadn't thought about what it would be like if she were dead—or worse, if she tried to kill Halle or me.

April offered an apologetic smile and cupped the boy's shoulders. "This is Connor. Annabelle Stephens was our first-grade teacher. She was the best. Right, Connor?"

He looked up at April. His eyes darkened with guilt. "She would have lived if she hadn't saved me."

April frowned. "She wanted it that way. Don't forget that. She loved you, and she wanted you to live. She would have done that for any one of you kids. We've discussed this, Connor. You can't blame yourself."

"What did you do," I asked, "when your parents changed and chased you?"

"Jenna!" Dad scolded.

Connor's eyes shot up to my dad and then back at me with a blank expression. "I ran."

After I finished my sandwich and chips and downed an entire bottle of water, I helped Dad fill up the empty bottles from the tap, and then we re-situated our packs.

The gunshots still continued, but they were infrequent, and I was beginning to get used to them.

Halle was playing with Madelyn and the younger boys while Connor seemed to prefer standing by the window and looking out of the holes.

Dad joined the adults to discuss what was next, but their conversation derailed somewhere between plans and theories to what had caused the virus.

"I'm just glad I never got a flu shot," April said. "There were reports that those who had one were turning faster once they were bit."

"I've heard that," Dad said. "I had mine, so if I get bitten, I guess you'd better shoot me quick."

"I didn't get mine, so let me say my good-byes," Tavia said, glancing back sadly at her son.

April scratched the back of her neck. "I still don't understand though. People with the flu shot are turning more quickly? After they've been bitten? After they die?"

Tavia leaned in closer. "The man on the news said that people who were bitten would get sick. They would run a high fever, vomit, and have headaches within the first hour. At first, they thought it was some kind of flu, so the doctors or whoever began looking at medical records. They were confused because those with the flu vaccination got worse and died quicker than those who hadn't gotten one."

April snorted. "You'd think when they came back and tried to eat people, the doctors would have figured out it wasn't the flu."

Tavia pressed her lips together. "That was early. It was right after they talked about the scientist. He did this. He created zombies, and now, we're all screwed."

April picked at her nails, nervous. "Do you think it's something in the vaccination?"

Dad shook his head. "No. I think, for whatever reason, the virus reacts with the vaccination. It's enzymatic, not the cause."

"Whatever that means," April said.

Dad grinned. "The flu shot isn't turning people into zombies. It just turns up the speed on the virus once you've been bitten."

"Oh," April said. "So, what caused it?"

Dad clenched his teeth. "The psycho scientist. He was probably obsessed with zombie movies and was just trying to see if he could make it a reality."

"We'll never know," Tavia said. "The only thing that matters is that he did it, and now, it's a reality for us all."

Tavia was right. The cause didn't matter, only that it was here, right outside the windows, and we were hiding from it, whispering to keep it from hearing us.

I used to do that when I was younger, when Mom and Dad were fighting. Dad was usually mad at me, and Mom would pick a fight with him just to keep him downstairs and out of my face. Since the divorce, he'd had a better handle on his anger, but I wondered how long he would last before he blew. We were all tired and exhausted and scared. None of those things made for a good combination for someone with so much rage boiling beneath the surface. Back then, I would hide from him in my closet. Now, we were hiding together—from something much worse.

I stood next to Connor, noting the wrinkles he made when he scrunched one eye while he looked out through a hole with the other.

"See anything?" I said quietly.

"Yes," he whispered. "I can see the cemetery from here."

I sighed and leaned against the thin plywood, looking up. "We're going to need something stronger to put on these windows."

"Yep."

The kids were at the table, coloring quietly. It seemed so easy for them to forget about the nightmare happening outside while they chose the perfect shade of blue and dragged it back and forth on the paper. I wished it were that simple, that I could just busy myself with something and pretend everything was normal.

I smirked and looked at Connor. "Are we running for our lives or running a daycare?"

He leaned away from the hole in the plywood and watched me for a moment, frowning. "If you saw inside the school, you wouldn't be complaining. Out of this entire town, only three of us are left. Another boy was in the church. His name was Evan. He was older than me, but he didn't make it out. So, now, it's just us and April. Your bunch brings the kid population to a grand total of eight. Eight—that's not even a daycare. That's just sad."

"I...I'm sorry. I was just trying to make conversation. I didn't mean—"

"I know," he said, looking back through the hole. "I didn't mean it either. I'm just mad."

I wondered what Connor was like before this had happened because he didn't act his age.
"I bet you are."

"If I were older, I could have saved more people. If I were older—"

"There are a lot of adults around. None of them have stopped this. Don't carry that around with you."

"I'm not carrying anything. The only things I have are my clothes."

"Where do you live? Maybe we could go get some of your things?"

He shook his head. "What does any of that stuff matter now?"

I shrugged. His way of thinking made me miss Chloe. I wondered where she was, if her mom had picked her up in time. I would hope. That was all I had left. "I wish I could have brought something from my old room. Makes it feel more like home." When Connor didn't respond, I continued, "It's not as loud as I thought it would be. Not a lot of screaming or hysterics. People get quiet when they're afraid."

"It's only been two days," Connor said without emotion. "Give them time."

"Halle used to talk all the time. She's barely said a word. She hasn't even really cried."

"Good. Loud kids get eaten."

"You're creepy," I said, crossing my arms.

He leaned back and looked at me, the corners of his mouth turned up ever so slightly. "You're weird."

"Yeah? Well, I'm not the one staring at a cemetery when dead people are walking around."

"I'm not staring at the cemetery. I'm watching Skeeter."

"Who's Skeeter?" I asked.

"The guy who saved me."

"I thought you said your teacher saved you?"

"He saved me from my teacher."

My eyebrows shot up. "Oh."

"He's burying his wife."

I furrowed my brows. "Oh."

"She was pretty. April said she said she was pregnant. I'm pretty sure he had to shoot her. It was…sad, I guess—if that's the right word."

"Sad is the right word."

"It doesn't seem like enough."

"May I?" I asked, pointing to the hole.

Connor wasn't imagining things. A man was standing in the cemetery with a shovel, and a body covered in plastic was lying on the ground next to him.

"I see him," I said.

"Yep."

The man was filthy, covered in sweat, and once in a while, he would pause to aim and fire his gun.

So, that's where the gunshots are coming from.

He was fearless, his shaggy sandy-blond hair sticking out of his ball cap. He was too far from me, so I couldn't make out his face, but his body would shake periodically, and I knew that he was crying.

"Should we tell him we're here? He seems like a good person to have around. Good with a gun," I asked.

"April already tried. He's going to find his brother and niece when he's done."

I looked at Connor. "I'm sorry about your parents and your teacher. That sucks—a lot."

"Yep," he said before walking away.

chapter eleven

"WHAT DO YOU MEAN, WE'RE NOT GOING?" I said, balling my hands into fists.

Dad and Tavia had pulled me into one of the bedrooms minutes after I'd woken up. A candle was the only light. The sun hadn't risen far enough from the horizon to light the cracks around the boarded windows. By their body language, I could tell this was a secret meeting, one that they were keeping from the younger kids.

Dad held up his hands, palms out. "Yet. I said, we're not going yet."

"Then, when?" I asked.

Tavia gestured for Dad to let her take over. "I understand that you want to get to your mom as soon as possible. I want you to, too. But we've had a long couple of days. We need to rest, eat, and make a plan. Then, we can decide from there."

"Decide what?" I asked.

Tavia reached out for me, but I pulled away.

"If we're going to try to walk the rest of the way."

"If?" I said, my voice getting louder. "Try?"

"Jenna," Dad said, "don't upset the kids."

"How many times do I have to say it?" I asked. "Mom is waiting on us. Every day we don't show up there, the more she worries. What if she's hurt? What if she needs our help? What if she's alone? She's only a few miles away!" I pointed at Dad. "You didn't let me catch her last time. I'm not letting you wait until she leaves again."

"What if she heads back this way?" Dad asked. "We would see her. We could bring her here."

My face fell, and I blinked, unimpressed with his ridiculous attempt to appease me with false scenarios. "You're scared. You're too scared to keep going."

"Honey," Dad began.

"You had to walk one day, and you're scared? You killed a dozen infected and walked away without a scratch. We hit a parked truck at fifty miles an hour and barely noticed. Why are you suddenly opposed to Red Hill?" I was trying to remain calm, but with every point, my tone got higher.

Tavia clasped her hands together. "We're all scared—"

"Then, stay!" I said, my voice transitioning to a weird chuckle even though I found none of what they were saying funny. "You don't have to come with us. But our mom is waiting for us at Red Hill, and that is where Halle and I are going."

"Not today," Dad said.

"Then, *when*?" I asked again, emphasizing each word.

"When I say," he said, sounding final.

I laughed once without humor. "I'm not asking to go to the mall. We're talking about *Mom* being *alone* without us! She's waiting for us! Do you honestly think I care that you're"—I used my fingers to make quotation marks in the air—"*the dad* right now?"

He stomped over to me and leaned into my face, taking me back to a time when my parents had still been married. "You'd better start caring. Just because it's the end of the world doesn't mean I won't whip your ass!"

Tavia pulled him back, and he flipped around, picking up a pillow and throwing it against the wall.

She eyed Dad warily. She was now seeing the side of him that Halle and I were used to, a side that I had been waiting for since this began.

"Andrew, maybe you should take a walk and see if you can do anything more to secure the house."

Dad turned to her, his face severe. The skin between his brows had formed a crevice, as deep and as dark as his anger in that moment. His hazel-green eyes burned bright against his olive skin. Just when I thought he would start yelling again, he left the room.

Tavia took a deep breath and held her hand to her heart. "That was—"

"Typical," I grumbled.

"You fight like that with him a lot?"

"We used to but not lately."

"He gets pretty mad, huh?" she asked, glancing at the closed door.

"He has a temper. He's working on it—allegedly."

"Is that why you want to get to your mom so bad?"

My eyebrows pulled in. "What would you do if you were separated from Tobin?"

She blinked.

"She's my mom. If I scrape my knee, I call for her. If I'm sick, I ask for her. If I'm scared, I cry for her. If there's an apocalypse,

I'm going to the ends of the earth for her." My eyes and nose burned. The sudden emotion surprised me. I wiped my cheek and sniffed, staring at the floor. "It's forty miles. We can make it."

"We…we don't know if Tobin can make forty miles. Who knows how long that would take on foot?"

"It doesn't matter if we waste time here. What were you two talking about? How to convince me to stay? For a few days? For a week? Forever?"

"No." She shook her head. "We're just worried about the little ones being able to make it that far. We need a car—or at the very least, a way to carry the supplies. I can't hold Tobin all day long. I can't run with him. It's too dangerous to try."

"I like you, Tavia. I'm not trying to be mean, but no one's asking you to come with us. If you want to stay here, stay here."

She was taken aback. "I know, but we can't do this alone. We need one another."

"Brad will leave eventually for Shallot. You need my dad to stay."

"It's not so different. You need him to leave."

"But he's *my* dad. I'm not going to give up on seeing my mom again because you can't travel with Tobin."

Tavia's sweet smile fell away. She wasn't being confrontational, but she did have the look of a mother bear protecting her cub. "Halle can't make the trip either. You would be risking her life if you go, especially if you try something as ridiculous as leaving without your dad. We're the adults, Jenna. He'll listen to me."

I took a deep breath and lowered my chin. Tavia was pretty intimidating. I thought about what Mom would say when I told her about this conversation later. She would want me to fight. She would want me to do anything I could to get Halle and me to Red Hill.

"My dad and I have had our ups and downs," I said, keeping my voice low and steady. "But if you try to make him pick between you or me, you'll lose."

I pulled open the bedroom door and walked out, passing the den where Halle and Tobin were sleeping soundly.

When I got to the kitchen, April was sitting at the rectangular table, sipping her coffee by candlelight. "Morning," she said, watching me with knowing eyes. "Your dad's outside."

"I know," I said, taking a seat at the opposite end of the table.

April's long hair was pulled up into a bun at the crown of her head. She had changed into an oversized white oxford and capri jeans with white slip-ons. She noticed me taking in her appearance, and she glanced down to her shirt. "It's Dean's. Probably weird, but I was looking through our closet for something to wear, and I just pulled it right off the hanger." I didn't respond. She continued, "I slept with a pile of his dirty clothes last night. Now, *that's* bizarre." She chuckled to herself and then began to cry.

Halle stumbled in with narrow eyes and wild hair, clumsily trying to put on her glasses as she made her way to the table.

"We've got to find you a brush," I said, pulling her onto my lap.

"What's for breakfast?" she said with a raspy voice.

Air so foul it should have been bright green wafted from her mouth to my nose, and in reaction, I turned my head.

"We've got to find you some toothpaste, too!"

She giggled and rested her cheek on my shoulder. Normally, she wasn't that affectionate with me. After Halle came home from spending the weekend at Dad's, she would wallow in Mom until she was finally ordered to bed, and even then, she'd ask for Mom to come to bed with her to snuggle. Dad wasn't an affectionate person by nature, so Mom had been the one who satisfied Halle's need for hugs, kisses, rocking, and holding. After Halle had come into the world, she had demanded everyone's attention, and I'd learned to live without it for the most part.

It occurred to me that Halle and I weren't really that affectionate at all, not since she was a toddler. Now, she was curled up in my lap like it was the most natural thing in the world.

"I can make you something," April said. "What would you like? The other kids will wake up hungry, too."

"Do you have biscuits and gravy?" she asked.

"I do," April said, standing.

I stood up, bringing Halle with me. "Come with me. We'll find a way to get all those rats out of your hair and some toothpaste."

"I don't have a toothbrush," Halle said.

I held up my index finger, making motions back and forth, while I bared my teeth.

"With my finger? No!" she whined.

"C'mon," I said, using her shoulders to guide her like Mom used to do.

We walked into the hallway to find the bathroom. I flipped on the light and closed the door.

April had given us the tour before bedtime the previous night, and I was glad that between eight kids and five adults, there was more than one bathroom. April had one in her room, too. She'd also said that because this room had only one window that was small and up high, it was okay to turn on the light but only during the day when the sun was bright, and it wouldn't draw attention.

The first drawer I pulled open had dozens of scattered ponytail holders, barrettes, and bows along with a comb and a brush. I imagined it was the bathroom where April would get her daughter ready.

Halle brushed her hair while I searched the other drawers. I found half a tube of toothpaste, a purple mermaid toothbrush, and a Spider-Man toothbrush. In the back of a drawer was a package of new toothbrushes. I was afraid if I asked, April would say no, so I opened the package, pulled out a toothbrush, and squeezed out a dab of the minty green gel.

"What are you doing?" Halle hissed.

"There are eight kids, and this package has four toothbrushes in it. Do the math," I said before scrubbing my teeth.

"You're stealing! At least ask!"

"Halle, you need to learn something right now. This is not going to be fixed tomorrow. Things are going to get worse, a lot worse, before they get better. You need to learn to take what you need now and say you're sorry later, especially if it's just a toothbrush!"

"No," Halle said, shaking her head. "We're not supposed to steal, especially not from people who are trying to help us."

"It's not stealing. It's borrowing."

Halle pressed her lips together, glaring at the toothbrush when I held it out to her. Her hair was brushed but poofy at the bottom and greasy at the roots.

"Brush your teeth," I demanded, pointing the toothbrush at her.

She grabbed it from me, holding it, while I squeezed the tube of toothpaste.

After a few spits into the sink, she rinsed out her mouth and wiped the water off with her arm.

I glanced at the overhead light. "I wonder how long the water and electricity will last?"

"What do you mean?" Halle asked, still frowning.

"It takes people to keep those things running. If everyone's infected, who's running it?"

"Everyone's *not* infected."

Someone knocked on the door, making us both jump.

"Are you about finished?" Connor asked, his voice muffled through the door.

"Coming right out!" I called, taking the toothbrush from Halle and corralling her to the door.

When I opened the door, I noticed that Connor had dark circles under his eyes, and his skin was pale, making his freckles stand out even more.

"Are you all right?" I asked.

"I didn't sleep great."

"Nightmares?" I asked.

"None of your business."

I stepped to the side and held Halle's shoulders as he passed by us and then shut the door.

"He's cranky in the mornings," Halle said.

"He misses his parents, and sometimes, it's easier to be angry."

We made our way back to the kitchen where April was spooning out gravy into bowls full of biscuits. Brad, Darla, Madelyn, and Logan were already seated, chatting about how good the food smelled.

Dad came in and locked the door behind him. The heaviness had left his face. "I found some metal posts we can use," he said to the adults. "We'll talk about it after breakfast."

April handed him a bowl.

"Thank you. Smells great."

"Here's a glass of juice," Tavia said, offering it to him.

"Thank you," he said, taking the drink and his bowl to the table.

As he sat down to eat, it occurred to me what a hot commodity he was. He wasn't ugly. He wasn't attached. He could shoot a gun and build things. Except for the fearless rifle-wielding widower who had been multitasking, taking out the undead while burying his wife, there was a very good chance that my dad was the only non-dead single male within miles. He might as well be Brad Pitt.

I tried not to throw up my breakfast. April and Tavia needed him, and they would make it really hard for him to want to leave. I had my work cut out for me, and I needed Halle on my side.

chapter twelve

"IT'S NOT THAT FAR," Brad said, trying to whisper. "We'll probably run out of gas halfway there. We'll walk the rest of the way."

I rubbed my eyes and blinked until my vision wasn't blurry anymore. All the adults were standing near the French doors in the back with Madelyn and Logan. Darla had worry in her eyes, but she was smiling.

"Brad," Dad said with concern in his voice, "I'm not trying to tell you what to do, but what's the rush? Let's try to get together some more gas for you, so you can make it the whole way—or at least most of it."

"What's going on?" I asked.

All heads turned in my direction.

Dad took a step toward me. "Nothing, honey. Go back to sleep."

I leaned to the side to look at Darla. "Are you leaving? You found a car?"

Her lips formed a hard line. She knew I'd be upset. They were trying to sneak out in the early morning with just enough light to be safe, so I wouldn't know.

"Jenna—" Dad began.

"Let's go with them," I said, suddenly wide-awake. "We can go with them!"

Dad shook his head. "The car they found is small. They only have enough room for them, and the more people they try to pack inside will take up that much more gas. They have less than a quarter of a tank, and they want to get to Darla's parents' house."

"But…" I looked at Darla, and she looked away. "Maybe…" My mind spun, trying to think of something. "Just take Halle and me. Take us as far as you're going, and we'll wait for Dad. When he gets there, we can figure out how to get the rest of the way."

"Jenna!" Dad scolded.

"I'll get our stuff together. Five minutes!" I said, turning on my heels.

Dad grabbed me. "Jenna, you're not going. You're staying here."

"But they've got a car. They'll be maybe five or ten miles from Mom!"

"We're sorry, sweetie. We just don't have room," Brad said.

I took a step back, holding my stomach. It felt like he'd just punched me there. "You can't leave without us," I begged. "It's been four days. She probably thinks we're dead. Please?"

"C'mon," Brad said, gathering his family.

"Good luck," Dad said.

"Wait!" I yelled, running into the kitchen. I ripped a piece of paper from one of the coloring books and wrote Mom a note in crayon.

In Fairview.
Will be there soon.
Don't give up on us.
Love you! Miss you!
Jenna

I handed the note to Darla.

She glanced at it and then threw her arms around me. "I'm so sorry!"

"Just...please give her the note if you see her. She might come into town for supplies."

Darla's lip trembled. "I..." She looked to her husband. "Brad, this is wrong. We should try to find a way."

Brad shook his head, sad. "You asked me to get you and the kids to your parents. This is how it has to be."

Darla looked down at the paper in her hand, folded it, and put it in her back pocket. "I will, Jenna. I promise."

I yielded, taking a step back, and watched them walk out the door. Blinking and looking up didn't stop the tears, and once they'd started, they wouldn't stop. I retreated to the bathroom, shutting myself inside. My entire body shook as I sat on the floor and sobbed into a folded towel. I didn't want to wake anyone. Halle didn't need to feel this kind of frustration and disappointment, too.

Thankfully, no one bothered me until Halle knocked on the door, needing to use the toilet. I washed my face with cold water, grateful it was still running, and I opened the door with a smile.

Even without her glasses, I couldn't fool my sister.

"What's wrong?" she asked.

I sighed. "I just miss Mom."

"Me, too," she said, throwing her arms around my pelvis.

I wasn't quite Tavia's height, and she was fairly short, probably five feet five inches. But Halle's forehead barely hit my belly button, and if I didn't bend down, she'd always end up hugging my butt.

I squeezed her back and stepped to the side, deciding to stay behind and help her get ready for the day. We hadn't left April's house, and it was easy to stop caring about things like showering or brushing our teeth. But I would keep reminding Halle that we should do it while we still had soap, shampoo, and toothpaste because one day very soon, we would miss them.

After breakfast, Dad slipped his backpack over his shoulders. When he went out, he'd typically keep his pack light, just enough to get him by if he were caught somewhere. I could tell more was inside the bag than a few bottles of water, a sandwich, and extra ammo.

"What are you doing?" I asked.

"Get your pack. You're coming with me."

"Why?" I asked.

He shrugged. "Okay, if you don't wanna go."

"I wanna go!" Halle said.

"I wanna go!" Tobin echoed.

I stared at him with a blank face. "What are you doing?" I asked again, emphasizing each word.

He glanced at April and Tavia, seeming nervous. They were making breakfast in the kitchen, peeking at him from over their shoulders. They didn't know either.

I picked up my bag, put two bottles of water inside with a package of crackers and a knife, and quickly threw it on. "Fine, let's go."

I grabbed Jud's aluminum bat sitting by the back door, and then we walked outside to the center of the fenced-in yard. I squinted from the bright sun. It was already hot.

Dad handed me a hat and sunglasses. "Here."

"Are you going to tell me where we're going?" I asked, pulling my dark hair through the hole in the back of the cap. The hat didn't sit right when I put on the sunglasses, so I pulled up the bill to sit higher on my forehead.

"Yes, we're going this way," he said, taking the first step.

I followed him out the gate and to the right, heading through backyards, until we reached the first road to the west. It was paved but not very well. Fairview only had a school because two rural towns had combined to form one. They had no hospital, no Walmart, not even a grocery store. But they had two banks and four churches.

Figures.

"I thought you might like to get out of the house," Dad said.

"Yeah, but that's not why you brought me with you. Everyone wants to get out of the house."

He looked both ways and then gripped the hammer in his hand. "I brought you for two reasons—to talk and to help. Did you see that church on the highway when we came into town? People were holed up in there the first day or two. I'm thinking it has supplies."

"If you want to go to the church, it's in the opposite direction."

"I don't want to lead any infected to the house, Jenna."

"They're not that smart. They don't know where you're coming from unless you get caught standing in the yard or they hear someone inside."

Dad sighed, annoyed. "You don't know that, Jenna."

"I've been right so far."

"Just…let's just go the long way to the church. Humor me."

"If it does have supplies, I bet Skeeter took them."

"What?"

"His name is Skeeter. Connor said he saved a bunch of people at the church, including Connor, but Skeeter lost his wife. He was burying her the last time I saw him."

"You saw him? When?"

"Through the hole in the plywood that Connor's always looking through. What does it matter?"

"Is he still around?"

"No. He went to go find his family."

Dad seemed comforted by that thought. He continued walking, keeping a watchful eye in all directions.

Infected were spread out—some of them standing in place, some of them stumbling around. None of them were closer than a block to us.

"What's wrong?" I asked.

"Just want to know who our neighbors are. Keep an eye on that one," he said, nodding to a woman in a black dress.

Her dark hair was long and tangled, and it dawned on me that while I was noticing her, she had noticed us, and she was now walking in our direction. A low moan came from her throat, her arms reaching toward us.

I gripped the bat, but I didn't panic.

"I worry about you," Dad said.

"Why?" I asked.

"You're thirteen, and you haven't really…you know, had a moment."

"I'm not talking about my period with you."

"No! No," he said, making a face. "I mean, you haven't seemed too upset by all of this. And that's concerning. It should be damn scary for a girl your age. It's scary to me."

"Maybe you just don't know me that well."

Dad pulled his mouth to the side, not amused.

I blew out a breath. I hated being too honest with him. It made me feel too vulnerable, like he would use it against me later. "I'm concentrating on getting to Mom. Once we get there, I'm not making any promises. I reserve the right to freak out at that point."

Dad picked up the pace, pointing to a few more infected who began to follow, too. "Jenna," he said, his tone a warning.

"Don't tell me that we might not make it to Red Hill. I won't accept that."

"No." He shook his head. "That is why I wanted to bring you with me. We're going to have to make a choice. If we go to Red Hill, the little ones can't make the trip."

"Halle can make it."

"Connor, yes. Halle, maybe. The other little ones, definitely not. Jud is barely five, and Tobin and Nora are practically toddlers. It's too far. We need to find a vehicle, a van, or maybe even two cars and gas that will get us at least most of the way there. If we can't…we'll have to leave them behind."

"I've already told Tavia that."

"You have?"

"Yes, and I'll tell April that, too. If they expect us to stay with them instead of being with our mom, they're crazy."

We crossed the highway, walking with purpose, and went past Brad and Darla's silver minivan and the green truck we'd crashed into. The church was just two blocks away on that side of the road. The first day when we'd arrived, it had been crawling with infected, but as far as I could tell, it was pretty much empty now. Dozens of bodies were lying on the back side of the church in line from the back door to the fresh grave Skeeter had dug.

"Skeeter must have cleared most of them before he left. He knew April was still here with her kids. Probably did it as a favor since he couldn't stay."

"Did she want him to stay?"

"Connor said she asked him to, but he said no."

Dad frowned.

I rolled my eyes. "No. Don't tell me."

"What?" he said, instantly defensive.

"Are you and April—"

"No," he said, tucking his chin and making the most ridiculous attempt to deny it.

He was a terrible liar. His eyes would glass over, and he'd blink a lot. That, and he had a whole lie face that he'd make.

My eyes and stomach rolled at the same time. "Gross."

"Don't ask if you don't wanna know," he said, positioning himself to swing if something came out of the back door.

"She just lost her husband. Her kids are in the house. It's just wrong."

"We all cope differently. Get ready."

I pulled up the bat, holding it in both hands.

Dad pushed open the door and then stepped back, waiting for something to jump out at us. When that never happened, he walked inside.

I glanced around me. A few infected were just walking into the church parking lot, a hundred or so yards away.

"Dad?"

He appeared in the doorway. "It's clear—for now. Let's get in and get out. The windows are wide open."

The room was dark, so I took off my sunglasses and perched them on the bill of my hat. Then, I stepped over the mess of bodies on the floor before shutting the door behind me.

Just inside the door, in a small kitchen in the back of the church, I saw a few cupboards. I found an open case of water, a big bag of chips, a mixed bag of apples and oranges, half a dozen cans of various vegetables, and cans of Spam.

It all went into my backpack, and then I walked down a hall before seeing a flight of stairs leading up to a doorway. Corpses of infected lay in a pile at the bottom, and a few were draped over the stairs.

"Should we check up there?" I asked.

"We're going to have to. They're coming in. Go. Go!" Dad ran past me to the top.

He opened the door, getting ready to swing at anything in his way. He checked behind the door and then motioned for me to follow him inside just as I heard infected pawing at the back door downstairs along with moans coming from another part of the church below.

Dad shut the door behind me, and I looked around. It was just one big room with a few tables, chairs, and a corkboard. There was also a television on a rolling stand and a gaming console. The walls were decorated with pictures illustrating stories from the Bible, from Jesus walking on water to Noah and the ark.

I laughed once.

"What?" Dad asked.

"They're all white."

"So?"

I shrugged. "I've just always thought that it's funny how all the people in Bible pictures are depicted as white. They weren't *all* white."

Dad glanced at me and laughed, shaking his head. "Don't let your grandma hear you say that."

He was right. Grandma was very strict on the way things happened in the Bible, history and science be damned.

We both chuckled until realizing at the same time that Grandma wouldn't hear me say that because Grandma was probably dead. My mom's mom was always serious about religion and church, and she'd tend to give Mom a hard time about everything. It just hit me that I'd probably never see her or Meme again. I might not see Chloe again. That freak-out that Dad and I had just discussed didn't seem so far away.

That was, until a sound from below had us scrambling over bodies on the floor to the already open window.

"I bet this is the window Connor came in and out of when they were here," I said, climbing out.

I looked down, seeing the AC unit. The infected were following each other to the back of the church, and there were more than before. When the moaning began, it was almost as if they were calling each other, signaling that there was food.

"We can make it, but we have to hurry," Dad said before jumping down.

He reached up for me, and I jumped down, too. We climbed down the unit together and ran across the street, retracing the route we'd taken to the church so that we wouldn't lead any infected to the house.

When we got to the school, I rested my hands on my knees. Dad kept an eye out while we caught our breath.

"My pack is heavier. I didn't account for that," I said. "If we end up on foot to Red Hill, we'll have to pack light."

"If we can get to Shallot, we can spend one night, leave there in the morning, and then make it to Red Hill by evening. I hope. I'm not sure."

"So, we're going?" I asked.

At the same time, a low moan sounded behind me, and something lunged at Dad from around the corner. I didn't look. I just swung my bat at what I thought to be at head level. It wasn't like the video games or television shows. I hadn't seen it coming. No scary music had built the suspense or indicated foreshadowing.

I could hear Dad struggling behind me, but all I could think about was the mouth belonging to the infected coming at me and keeping it away from my skin. The adrenaline made everything both sharp and blurry. In one moment, I was next to its bloodstained clothes and dry, scratchy skin, and the next, it was standing in front of me, reaching out again. I wasn't quite sure how I'd gotten away.

He was tall. I couldn't kick his knees out from under him, so I swung the bat as hard as I could. That wasn't like the video game either. The vibration from the impact traveled up the bat and into my arms, startling me, but the creature fell, and I swung at his head.

The bat met his skull with a crack, but I didn't stop until the bone gave way.

Dad grabbed my collar, and we ran south—away from the school, away from the house. The groans from the infected had attracted more.

"We've got to lead them away from the house!" Dad said. "This way!"

We sprinted through backyards, hopped over fences, and dodged plastic pools and swing sets until we made a full circle, sneaking into April's backyard once we were sure it was clear.

"Oh," I said, noticing Dad was covered in dark goo.

"I panicked," he said. "I was trying to get him off me, so I could help you."

"I held my own," I said.

"I noticed. You weren't bit?" he asked.

"No," I said, shaking my head. "You?"

Until that moment, I hadn't been truly afraid. I hadn't realized that something as simple as a bite could take Dad away from me. He would die, and Halle and I would be on our own.

He pulled open the back door of April's house, and once it was closed behind us, he hugged me, and I sobbed into his chest.

chapter thirteen

TAVIA FANNED TOBIN, who was playing quietly on the floor. She had already tried to turn on the television in hopes that basic cable might have the smallest bit of news, but every channel was snow.

We had been at April's for nearly a month. Almost a week after we had fled Anderson, we had been putting together a puzzle on the floor when we heard a loud boom, and the house had even shaken a bit. Dad had run outside, afraid the military were bombing the cities, but all we had seen was a thick black pillar of smoke.

After that, aside from that, life had consisted of trying to keep the kids quiet when an infected wandered close and fighting boredom. Dad had been trying to convince April and Tavia to help him clear out the school, so we could move there, but they were afraid the effort and risk wouldn't be worth it. April had argued that there were too many windows to secure. After they had returned from a scouting trip, Tavia had reasoned that the three of them would quickly be overtaken by the number of infected children and the few adults who were still inside. She didn't think she could bring herself to kill them, no matter how desperate we were for shelter and despite the many times Dad and I had tried to convince her that they were already dead.

Neither of them knew that Dad was trying to help them find something more secure if we couldn't find a vehicle for everyone—and we hadn't yet.

Summer was in full swing. By mid-morning, we would be sweating. By some miracle, we still had electricity, but April was afraid to turn on the air conditioning. She was worried that when the outside unit kicked on, the noise would draw the infected. She was right, but with no air conditioning and no open windows, the house had become stuffier with each passing day. Dad had scavenged several box fans and a single tall oscillating fan, which helped with the heat.

The younger kids were becoming depressed, getting turned down every time they'd beg to go outside and play. We were all afraid their giggling and screams would attract the infected, and if we took the kids away from the house, we would get into trouble and be too far from safety. Dad and I would try to bring back a new toy every time we went out to keep the kids busy and happy.

I was more worried about the food situation. April's once-packed pantry was looking sparse. The adults had talked about rationing. Dad and I would rummage through the houses in the tiny town every day. We only had a few houses left to search, and a lot of the food we'd found was spoiled.

"Are you going out today?" Connor asked, watching me fold towels with a bored look on his face.

"For food? I don't know," I said. "Dad hasn't mentioned it."

"I've gotta get out of this house. I want to go with you next time."

I looked over at Dad, who was sitting on the floor with April, Nora, and Tobin. Jud was walking around them, patting their heads, while calling each of them a duck.

"Goose!" Jud said when he patted Dad's head.

Dad scrambled up and tried to catch him before Jud got to his spot, but Dad wasn't trying very hard.

Tavia was napping in the recliner, in and out of consciousness.

"It's dangerous, Connor. It's not an errand."

"I know. I was thinking maybe...that maybe your dad would teach me how to shoot a gun."

I snorted. "He won't even teach me."

"Maybe he should."

I stopped folding towels and watched as Dad tapped April on the head and called her a goose. They ran around the circle as the kids laughed hysterically.

"I'll talk to him," I said.

"Good." Connor went back to his window, watching the world go on without us.

April clapped once and stood, directing all the kids to the bathrooms to get ready for bed.

Within the hour, the candles were blown out, and the kids were tucked in. I sat next to Halle while she lay in bed next to Tobin.

"Do you remember how we used to find songs on the radio when Mom picked us up after school, and we would sing them really loud?" I asked. "Mom would roll down the windows and sing with us, and people would look at us like we were crazy."

Halle giggled. "And we would bounce our heads and dance! That was fun. I miss school."

"Me, too," I said. Mostly, I just missed Chloe.

I waited for Dad to kiss her good night, and then I followed him into April's bedroom.

She was taking a shower. We were alone.

"Connor made a good point today," I said, watching Dad turn down the covers.

"About what?" He had a smirk on his face. He already knew I had an agenda.

"He mentioned you taking us out and teaching us how to shoot."

Dad's face twisted into confusion, like I'd just spoken a foreign language. Whatever he had expected, it wasn't that.

"It's a reasonable point. If you're taking me out with you, I need to know how to use a gun—not just to defend myself, but to also keep from shooting anyone I don't want to shoot."

"No, Jenna. You're not old enough."

"I'm old enough to go out scavenging with you. I took out that zombie a couple of days ago."

"That was your second one."

"So? What does that have to do with learning how to shoot?"

"It's a gun," he said, already getting flustered, "and you're thirteen."

"Why does it matter how old I am? Dead people are walking around outside."

Dad glared at me. "You're not ready."

"*You're* not ready."

"No, I'm not."

"That's an emotional response, and emotion is irrelevant."

"Says who?" he asked. "And stop talking like you're a forty-year-old psychologist. It's creeping me out."

"Connor needs to learn, too."

"He's Halle's age, Jenna! You think Halle could handle a gun? Or should?"

"You're not listening. It's been a month."

"Not this again."

"You said we were going to find Mom. You said, if we didn't find a vehicle as of a week ago, we would leave. That was supposed to happen yesterday. Why are we still here?"

"Because we're not ready. Your sister is not ready."

"She's waiting on us," I said, a ball forming in my throat.

"You're starting to sound like a CD on repeat, Jenna, and I'm getting really tired of the song."

I rolled my eyes at his analogy. Nobody used CDs anymore.

"When we're out there, I might need more than a baseball bat. What if something happens to you? You can't always be there to protect us. You have to teach me how to protect Halle."

Dad's face flushed. "Enough, Jenna."

"And Connor. If he's going to be the man of the house once we leave, he needs to know how to use a gun."

"You're leaving?" April said from the doorway. A yellow towel was wrapped around her, and water dripped from her hair.

Dad looked like he'd been caught, and he stuttered, "She's…she's just arguing."

"You're going to leave us here?" April said, her eyes wide.

"No!" Dad said, but his lie face betrayed him.

"Just you and the girls? Is it because you want to be with Scarlet?"

"April, honey, that's not it," Dad said, walking around the foot of the bed.

"Then, why would you need to leave us behind? I don't understand," she said, her voice cracking.

"Jenna," he snapped, "go to bed."

My shoulders fell, and I walked to the couch in the living room where I'd been sleeping for four weeks. Every night, I would lie there, hoping that it would be our last, that Dad would decide the next day that it was time to go. At the same time, I would be terrified of being on foot and getting caught out in the open without shelter. We wouldn't have the safety and routine of April's house, and I'd worry about how Halle would do between here and Red Hill. But we were running out of food, and this many of us in one house was a burden on everyone.

Dad and April's tense conversation was muffled by the walls, but I could still hear them.

I sighed.

"Didn't go so well?" Connor asked.

"April knows we're leaving."

"Everyone knows you're leaving."

"They do?"

"We're not stupid. You want to be with your mom. You should be with your mom. April's just scared and maybe being a little selfish."

"Then, why did she act so surprised?"

"Maybe she was hoping he would change his mind."

Guilt settled in, making me kick off the sheet and sit up. I pulled my knees to my chest. "I don't want anything to happen to any of you, but…it's not…we can't—"

"Your mom is more important. I get that, and April gets that even though she doesn't want to admit it. She has kids. She wouldn't want to be separated from them, and she knows the little kids can't make the trip."

"You could," I said.

He sighed. "Someone has to stay here and help. They can't do it on their own."

I lay back down, turning on my side and using my bent arm as a pillow.

Dad's and April's voices had turned sweeter and less angry. He was defusing the situation, which wasn't like him at all. Soon, it quieted down, and Connor's breathing slowed to a relaxing rhythm. My eyes grew heavy, and after a few slow blinks, I was out.

April, Dad, and Tavia were sitting at the kitchen table, having a low conversation, when my eyes finally peeled open. The sun was shining through where the plywood met the windowsill. The windows were now fortified with wooden planks that Dad had nailed to the wood bordering the glass.

I lay still, trying to hear what they were saying, but it was no use. Whatever they were talking about, none of them were happy.

Finally, I sat up and invited myself to the table. In unison, they all sat back against their seats, realizing how rigid their postures had been.

"What's going on?" I asked.

April didn't take her eyes away from Dad. "We're discussing your departure."

Tavia looked down at the table, her nostrils flaring.

Dad shifted nervously in his chair. "April will allow us to stay a few more days. In return, you and I will gather more supplies for them and teach her and Connor how to use a gun."

"Wait, what?" I said, instantly incensed. "You're kicking us out with conditions?"

April tried to retain her reserve. "I'm not kicking you out, Jenna. You want to leave, don't you?"

"Yes, but this is extortion."

Tavia looked up at me then. "Jenna, you want to get to your mother. We all understand that. But we are being left here to fend for ourselves—"

"Which you would be doing anyway!" I interrupted.

"Jenna," Dad chided.

Tavia continued, "To fend for ourselves, so we need to get everything in line in order to do that the best way we can. We're two women with three small children to feed and protect. We're just trying to do our best to keep everyone safe."

"You're two women who have been depending on my dad and me to do all the heavy lifting while you sit in the safety of this home and keep the kids entertained."

Tavia raised an eyebrow. "You've been living in April's home and eating her food, too, young lady."

"And where do you fit into all of that, Tavia?" I seethed. "What have you done besides babysit?"

Dad held up his hands. "All right, all right. I'm going to teach April and Connor how to shoot. Jenna, I'm also going to teach you."

I blinked.

"You and I are going to do one last sweep of the entire town to make sure April, Tavia, and the kids have plenty of supplies, including seeds and equipment for planting, and then we'll be on our way."

I crossed my arms. "You were planning to do that anyway—without the threat," I said, glaring at the women. "And just so you know, he has scoured this whole town trying to find a vehicle or two vehicles to fit us all. He hates that he has to leave you behind, but he knows the kids can't make the trip! And you're treating him like a traitor!"

Tavia and April looked down, unable to respond. I was fully aware that I was in the middle of a juvenile temper tantrum, but I was allowed to behave like a thirteen-year-old on occasion, especially when people were being mean to my dad. That was my job.

Dad stood. "Okay then, we should get started."

chapter
fourteen

I DOUBLE-KNOTTED HALLE'S SHOES and tightened the straps on her backpack. "You're sure it's not too heavy? We've got a long walk today and an even longer one tomorrow."

"I'm sure," she said, pushing up her glasses. "I can do it."

I winked at her. "I know you can. Just don't want you to wear out too fast."

Dad had his hiking pack on, complete with the tent on top—just like he'd worn five weeks ago, that Friday when we'd last seen our mom. Dad's skin was tanned from spending time outside in the summer sun, and he now had more scruff on his face than I'd ever seen. I wondered if Mom looked any different—or if Halle or I did.

As scared as I was to start the journey, not knowing what was between here and there and not sure how Halle would do, the thought of finally being on our way to get to Mom surpassed all my fears and trepidation.

Halle was in a good mood, too. It had taken a long time for both of us to fall asleep the night before. It all reminded me of what it had felt like on the first day of school. I was sure it would be a lot like that, too. When the excitement wore off, it would be torture just to get through the day, running into bullies and being exhausted by the end of the day. Mom would be like summer break.

I put a hat on Halle's head. Dad hugged Tavia and Tobin, and Jud and Nora, and then he shook Connor's hand. He kissed April, who wiped a tear that had escaped down her cheek.

Despite the fact that we'd become enemies fighting over my dad since we arrived, I hugged Tavia and April, too. They'd been our family for a time, and Tavia was a big reason we'd survived the first day.

I knelt down in front of Tobin and gave him a hug.

He squeezed me back. "Bye-bye, Jenna," he said, wiping his nose with the top of his wrist.

He still had his train in his pudgy palm. His hair had grown out to a cute puffball. I wasn't sure if I'd just tried not to think about it or if I had just been too focused on leaving, but it was the first time I realized that Tobin wasn't coming with us. It was devastating.

That was why Dad had taken so long to make his decision. He'd known it would feel like this. He'd known what it would mean for us to leave them behind. I had been too focused on Mom to even think about it. Now that it was here and I understood, I needed to say my good-byes and leave. It was an awful, horrible situation, but it was always going to end this way.

I hugged him again and kissed his cheek, and then I hugged Nora and Jud. Connor, always stoic, barely seemed to notice that we were saying good-bye, but I hugged him anyway even though he didn't hug me back.

"I'll miss you," I said, wiping my cheeks.

Dad opened the door, looked out, and then turned back one last time. "Take care."

Halle and I followed him out the door, and we walked in a line—Dad first, Halle in the middle, and I brought up the rear, just like we'd discussed. In my right hand, I held the aluminum bat Jud had given me as a going-away present. Dad's rifle was hanging from a strap on my shoulder. I had gotten a lot of practice over the past forty-eight hours, and I was a decent shot, but Dad had said the hardest part was knowing what to do under pressure. I hoped that I would make him proud.

The sky looked like a watercolor painting. Blues, purples, pinks, and yellows were bursting from the horizon as the sun erupted and lit up the sky. The crickets and cicadas chirped and buzzed in the background as the grass hissed under our feet with each step.

We reached Kellyville just inside of two hours. Rotting bodies were lying flat in the grass and in the streets and hanging over porch railings. Vacant cars were everywhere, and Dad checked each one for keys. He even searched a few of the bodies nearby for keys. The infected had moved on, so I took special care in looking for any signs of life in the houses, but I found nothing—no curious eyes peeking out from covered windows, no women trying to flag us down.

"It's completely empty," I said.

"Looks that way. Let's keep moving," Dad said.

Just twenty minutes after we'd left the city limits of Kellyville and turned north onto Highway 123, Halle made the first comment. I was surprised she'd lasted that long.

"My feet hurt," she said. "My toes are rubbing."

"Your feet are growing," Dad said. "We'll have to find you some bigger shoes."

We tried to keep her mind off the hike, but another twenty minutes later, she whined again, "I'm hungry."

"Already?" Dad asked.

"Yes. Can we get a snack?" she said.

"Not yet," Dad said. "We have to walk for five and a half hours today, remember? Another hour, and we'll be more than halfway done for the day. That'll be lunchtime."

"That's going to take forever," she grumbled.

"We're more than halfway to lunch, if you can think about it that way," I said.

"Really?" she asked.

"Really," I said.

At lunchtime, we found a shaded spot that had a little bit of elevation, so we could see if anything was coming. Dad unfolded the paper towels and handed us our sandwiches, and I divvied out the water.

"Look at that," Halle said, pointing to the sky.

The pillar of smoke was still billowing from something, but now, it was white instead of black.

"Is that Shallot?" I asked.

Dad looked up. "No, it's too close. Shallot is farther away."

I stared up at it, squinting against the sun. "It's been burning for a long time."

Dad shrugged. "It's not burning. The smoke is white. It's smoldering. Debris from an explosion can smolder for months."

"What do you think exploded?" I asked.

"Most likely, something made of metal. I guess we'll find out when we pass by it," he said.

Halle was surprisingly upbeat. "When we see Mom, I'm going to hug her first, okay, Jenna? I got dropped off at school first, so it's been longer since I've seen her."

"Good point," I said. "Okay, you can hug her first."

Dad winked at me.

"And I'm going to sleep with her the first night," Halle proclaimed.

"Where am I going to sleep?" I asked.

"I don't know. I don't remember the farmhouse that well. I bet the doctor has a couch."

"What if I want to sleep with her, too?" I asked.

Halle made a face. "Where are you going to sleep, Daddy? Will you and Mom get married again?"

Dad nearly spit out his water. "Your mom and I are friends. I think we get along better that way, don't you? We can still all live together at the farmhouse."

"Do you think anyone else is there?" I took a bite of my sandwich.

"What do you mean?" Dad asked.

"Like, maybe the doctor. It is his house, and it's a good place to go. Maybe his family is there. He has two daughters, but they have boyfriends," I said, feeling inclined to warn him.

He chuckled. "I think I'll live."

"What if someone else came along whom Mom liked? What if she's there with him? Kind of like you and April?" I asked, not really expecting an answer.

Halle giggled, and Dad began to pack up.

"All right, girls. Lunch break is over. We have another few hours to walk, and we need to find a good place to set up camp unless we come across a house. Keep your eyes open."

"What?" Halle asked, frozen.

Dad stood, looking down at her. "We need to find a safe place to set up the tent."

"We're sleeping outside?" she asked, her eyes wide. She actually began to tremble at the thought. "I don't want to, Daddy. I want to sleep with Mom tonight."

Dad offered an apologetic half smile. "We're not going to make it to Red Hill tonight, Pop Can. We'll make it most of the way to Shallot before dark. We'll set up camp, and then we'll walk again tomorrow. It'll be okay. Jenna and I are going to take turns keeping watch, and it's a full moon, so we'll be able to see before anything gets too close."

She shook her head. "No. No, Daddy."

Dad hugged her. "I won't let anything happen to you, Halle. I promise."

He helped her put on her backpack, and then we set out again, walking down the hill. We returned to the road, heading north on Highway 123. The tune began to play in my head, Halle's high-pitched voice singing her made-up song, as it did every time I thought about the directions Mom had taught us.

123? 123!

We crossed the paths of just a few infected and one small group of four or five, and we had no trouble either sneaking past them or waiting while Dad took them out. The sun bore down on us, and every part of my exposed skin was turning pink and feeling raw. We had less than half a bottle of sunscreen, and Dad and I had agreed that Halle's pale skin would need it more than either of us, who tended to tan instead of peel.

By late afternoon, we still hadn't found a good place to camp, so we continued on. I was beginning to wonder if Dad was hoping to come across a house, but I didn't remember anything but pasture and cattle being between Fairview and Shallot.

I ended up putting on Dad's pack and carrying mine, so Dad could give Halle a piggyback ride for a few miles. The sun was getting lower in the sky, and I was getting nervous.

"Dad?" I said finally.

"I know."

"It's getting late."

"I know."

We walked another two miles, and I wrinkled my nose. "What is that?"

Halle held her wrist to her face. "Ugh! What is that smell?"

Dad stopped abruptly. "I don't believe it."

Halle peeked over his shoulder. "What is that?"

I caught up to him and stood there with my mouth hanging open. On the top of a hill was a rock that said *Shallot*.

"We made it. We're here," Dad said.

"Look," Halle said, pointing to the sky. "The white smoke is from here."

Dad's expression changed from surprise to relief to intenseness. "The hill is obscuring what could be on the other side. I don't know what the smoke is about. If Shallot has a lot of infected, we might have to run or act quickly. Jenna, don't shoot unless it's absolutely necessary. We don't want to draw attention to ourselves. You have to do what I say, when I say. Understood?"

Halle and I agreed, and Dad set her back on her feet.

I gripped Halle's hand. "Don't let go, no matter what."

Halle nodded, worry beginning to shadow her face. We had no clue what we were walking into. Shallot was about the same size as Fairview. A stalled car was on the highway, and there was no way to know how many people had stopped here on their way to wherever.

I hoped that we would run into Brad and Darla right off the bat, and then they could take us to where they were staying.

Dad walked along the road into town. We had barely reached the other side of the hill with the rock before Dad hissed at us to hide. We retreated behind a tree, standing behind Dad, and he peeked out from behind it.

"Damn it," he whispered. "It's overrun."

"Why does it smell like that?" I asked, my face twisting into disgust. It was the worst thing that had ever hit my nose. It was like charred dirty feet, skunk, and musk all rolled into one.

Dad's eyes danced around, taking everything in. "Smells like a bloater."

"A what?"

"A decomposed body after it catches fire. They are full of bacteria and built-up gases. When they catch fire, it releases that into the air. I think some of the infected must have either been caught in the explosion or walked into the fire."

"Let's go," Halle whispered. "I don't want to stay here."

"We can't make it to Red Hill before dark," I said.

"Agreed," Dad said. "We'll just walk down this road and try to get into the first house we see. We'll be sure to sneak in undetected, so that means quickly and quietly."

"Okay, Dad," Halle said in her small voice.

"Let's go," he said softly.

We stuck to the trees and then went down the back alley of a line of houses.

Dad hopped the chain-link fence of a two-story house that already had wooden slats on the windows. He tried to open the back door, but it was locked.

A familiar low moan sent a shiver up my spine, and I pulled Halle closer, looking all around. I couldn't see it, but it had seen us—or maybe he could *smell* us.

Dad went to the next house, also a two-story. The outside slats had been painted dark green, and the windows had hideous brown shutters. The back door opened immediately. He disappeared inside for a bit and then came back out, waving at us. I helped Halle over the fence, and then I hopped over myself. We began to run to the back door.

A moan sounded from the fence, and I turned. An infected, a man in overalls, was reaching for us over the chain-link fence. I looked to Dad, who was signaling frantically for me to come inside, but I knew if we left that thing at the back fence, it would alert others to food, and we would be in real danger, real fast.

I held the bat low in both hands, twisting my palms on the grip, as I walked over to the infected.

"Jenna!" Dad hissed.

I took the first swing, stunning the creature. A month's worth of decay had made him squishier, his skin and muscles not protecting his bones. I hit him again, and he fell.

"What are you doing? Get your ass in here!"

I jumped over the fence and hit him two more times until he stopped reaching out for me. I nudged him with my foot and then hopped back over the fence. I ran at full speed to the door as if something were after me. I closed the door behind me, my heart trying to beat out of my chest.

"What were you doing?" Dad growled. "Trying to get yourself killed?"

"They call to each other," I said. "If I had left him out there, he would have drawn others here, and if enough came, they could knock over the fence and get inside the house."

Dad was taken aback. He thought about that for a moment. "Good call, kiddo. Just…be careful. I'm going to have a coronary before we get to Red Hill. Do you know what your mother would do to me if I showed up without you?"

"Let's just not do that, okay?" I said with a smile, still breathing hard.

Dad hugged me tight. He took in a deep breath and then kissed my hair. "I'm glad you're with me, kid."

chapter fifteen

DAD IMMEDIATELY BEGAN CHECKING THE LOCKS on the front and back doors, and then he looked for materials to fortify the windows. We searched every room for something, anything to keep the infected from breaking through. We had no luck with wooden slats like the ones on the church or plywood sheets like the ones at April's. So, we used furniture and made sure all the curtains were drawn.

"No flashlights or candles unless absolutely necessary," Dad said. "Keep your voices low. We just need to keep them out for the night."

"I don't like this house," Halle whined.

Dad gently touched her cheek with his fingertips. "We'll just sleep upstairs. I'll put breakables at the top and bottom of the stairs. If anything knocks into them, we'll hear."

Halle's bottom lip trembled.

I went into the kitchen to look for food, and when I opened the pantry door, I gasped. "Dad!" I whispered as loud as I dared. "Dad!"

He rushed in, dragging Halle with him. Surprise brightened his face. "Whoa!"

The pantry was stocked with cans of fruit and vegetables, rice, potted meat, potato chips, peanut butter, pickles, and bottled water. There were two loaves of moldy bread and rotted fruit as well, but I couldn't stop staring at the potatoes. I reached in and gave one a squeeze.

"They're still good!" I picked up a package of powdered gravy. "Mashed potatoes and gravy!"

Dad opened the refrigerator. "I don't believe it. They still have electricity!"

"Then, I bet Mom does, too!" Halle pushed up her glasses and showed off her oversized teeth.

We spent the evening cooking and whispering, discussing how Mom would react when we showed up the next day at Red Hill. Dinner consisted of mashed potatoes and Spam, both drenched in dark gravy, and green beans. We hadn't eaten this well in weeks.

"I wish we could take this pantry with us," I said. "We don't know what they'll have left at the ranch."

Dad paused. "Maybe I should go get her, along with anyone else there, and bring them back here. We can come back to get you and load up on supplies."

"You don't think they do that once in a while anyway?"

Halle's eyes bulged, and her mouth formed an O. "What if they did that tomorrow, and we didn't have to walk to Red Hill alone?"

"That," I said, "would be the best luck we've had in a long time."

Dad snorted. "If they have a scavenging party, I don't think your mom would be on it."

"Why not? I'm on yours," I said.

"Your mom's not really the type," Dad said.

"Neither am I."

"Okay, okay," he said. "I just can't imagine her bashing in skulls on her way to Shallot to pick up supplies. But you're right. We're in different times."

Halle's grin faded. "Is that what we're going to have to do? Bash in skulls to get to Red Hill?"

"No, honey. I'm sorry," Dad said, realizing his mistake too late. "I was just teasing Jenna about your mom. I wasn't being serious."

But that was our reality now, and we all knew it was a possibility even if Dad didn't want to admit it.

"There are so many infected in town. Shallot's even smaller than Fairview. I don't get it."

"I don't know," Dad said before shoveling a bite of potato into his mouth.

After dinner, we all pitched in to clean up, and then Dad and I moved a desk to the bottom of the stairs before covering it with drinking glasses and some jars I'd found on the top shelf of a cabinet. We dragged two nightstands from one of the bedrooms to the top of the stairs before covering it with decorative vases and figurines.

I looked in all the closets for clothes my size, but I had no luck. I thought I found Halle a pair of shoes, but when I called her in to try them on, they were too big.

"I don't want to put my shoes back on," Halle said, disappointed.

"You don't have to tonight. Just be sure to keep them together by the bed in case we need to put them on fast."

She looked longingly at the bigger shoes. I felt so sorry for her. I pulled off her socks and began rubbing her feet. Her big toes were red and angry. We would have to find her new shoes sooner rather than later.

She leaned back on her hands and grinned. "You are the bestest sister ever."

"You're not kidding. Your feet don't smell the greatest, and they're...moist."

Halle giggled, and I giggled with her.

Dad stood in the doorway, smiling at us. "All right, let's get showered and in bed before dark. No lights, remember?"

We stood and made our way to the bathroom. The situation struck me as funny. Five weeks ago, Halle would have pitched a fit and begged to stay up. But without a television or toys to play with, there was nothing to stay up for.

I scrubbed my body and then helped Halle. We rinsed off a day's worth of road dirt and sweat and then dried off before getting dressed again. I hated getting clean and then putting on my smelly clothes, but without the windows boarded, it was too risky to try to wash clothes and hang them to dry.

I collapsed on the queen-sized bed next to Halle. Dad had pulled a twin-sized mattress from the other room and laid it on the floor next to our bed. Dad wanted us all to have plenty of room while we slept, so we would be well-rested the next day.

We all lay in the dark, waiting to fall asleep. It was too quiet again. The old house creaked and made noises we weren't used to. Every time something cracked or knocked, Dad would hold his breath and listen before relaxing again.

Halle was too exhausted to worry, and she fell asleep within minutes. She began to snore, and I turned on my side to face Dad, bunching up the down pillow under my arm. The bed was much more comfortable than April's couch.

"What's the plan for tomorrow?" I whispered. "You're not serious about going on without us?"

"I don't know. What do you think?"

His question took me off guard. I wasn't used to him asking for my opinion on anything.

"Uh...let's weigh the pros and cons."

"Sounds good."

I thought for a moment. "You could travel faster without Halle. You could maybe get there and back if Mom has her car and, by some miracle, still has gas."

"Let's not bet on that. We're talking about you and Halle being here alone for at least one full night, and that's if everything went perfectly."

"That's a scary thought. We could do it though, especially if we found something to cover the windows."

"How important is it to you that we leave tomorrow?" he asked. "If we take the time to prepare, I could fortify the windows downstairs. I might even be able to find a car with gas. We could drive out of here and be at the ranch in fifteen minutes."

I sighed. I was frustrated with the choice, but that was only because the smart thing to do meant not seeing Mom the next day. She was only about fifteen miles away. Knowing we were so close was maddening.

"We have to at least find something to reinforce the windows," I said, defeated.

"Your birthday is in five weeks," Dad said.

"Yeah? That means we missed the Fourth of July, not that we had fireworks," I said without emotion.

Birthdays and holidays didn't mean what they used to. From now on, it would just signify another year of survival.

"My daughter will be fourteen. Hard to believe," he said before taking in a slow deep breath.

"Harder to believe than a zombie apocalypse?" I said with a smirk he couldn't see.

I could hear him scratching at his beard. "I promise that you'll spend your birthday with your mom, Jenna. How about that?"

A smile crept across my face. "That would be the best present you could give me. That, and you shaving."

"Done," he said. "Now, get some rest. We have a lot of work to do tomorrow."

I nodded and closed my eyes.

chapter sixteen

DAD HAD BEEN GONE FOR HOURS when I saw him. A dirty large man was walking down the road, but he wasn't shuffling. He was alive. Part of me wanted to yell out from the second-story window, to pound on the glass until he looked up, but I didn't know who he was.

This far into a worldwide disaster, people who had once been civil became desperate to survive. That meant stealing and robbing and doing other things that I didn't want to think about. The man below could be helpful, or he could take all our food—or worse.

I let him walk by, and then I searched the streets again for my dad, letting my eyes skip over all ages of infected ambling about.

"I'm hungry," Halle said, tugging on my shirt. "And I'm mad."

"Why?" I asked, turning to see the sour look on her face.

"We were supposed to see Mom today," she said, trying to keep the whine from her voice and the tears from her eyes.

"I know. I wanted to see her today, too. But we were surprised to see this many of those things in Shallot, and it made us wonder how many might be between here and the ranch. We have to have a plan, Halle. We're almost there. We don't want to make a mistake when we've come this far, right?"

She pulled her mouth to the side. "I guess."

"I'm disappointed, too. It's hard being this close and not just going to see her. But she is going to be so happy to see us. We have to concentrate on that."

Halle could no longer keep the tears from her eyes. "I'm going to be happy to see her, too!" She threw her arms around me, and I hugged her. "I miss her so much, Jenna! I want Mom!"

"Me, too," I said, feeling my own lip quivering. "We just have a few more things to do, and then we can go. But for now, let's scrape up some lunch. Dad will be really hungry when he gets home."

Halle lifted her glasses and wiped her eyes. I looked out the window again, and I saw the man walking back by. He had a bag with several gun barrels sticking out of the top. He wasn't searching. He knew exactly where he was going. I watched him until he disappeared under the awning of the house on the next block. It was the last house on the road. I swallowed and then let Halle pull me down the stairs.

As I put a pot of ravioli on the cooktop, the back door opened and closed. I scrambled for Dad's rifle and stood in front of Halle, cocking it at the same time.

"Good girl," Dad said. "Don't waste time asking who it is."

I blew out a breath of relief. "You scared the crap out of me."

Dad raised an eyebrow, putting down all the plastic sacks in his hands. "The undead are walking around outside, and I scared you?"

"A guy was walking around outside," I said.

"Lots of guys are walking around outside," he said, absently digging through his sacks.

"No, like a real guy, an alive guy. He walked down to that brick house we couldn't get in, and then he walked back down the street to the house on the end of the road by the pasture."

Dad froze. "What did you do?"

I shrugged. "I did nothing. I didn't recognize him, and Halle and I were alone. What took you so long?"

"He's living at the end of the street? What was he doing in the brick house?"

"He was packing a lot of guns. I think he found them at that house. He didn't see us. I don't think he knows we're here."

Dad let the air escape that he'd been holding. "Good. That's good. We should be more careful. I'm glad I have smart kids."

"Are you going to answer my question?"

"Oh, I had to find something to carry back the plywood. I found a lumberyard and a tiny general store that was mostly empty."

"You have blood on your shirt," I said, looking at him more closely. "And your face."

Dad looked down and then reached into his pocket. He handed me a piece of paper. It was my note to Mom that I had given to Darla.

"Where did you get this?" I asked, excited. "Did you see Brad and Darla?"

Dad lowered his eyes, his face solemn.

My hand went up to my mouth. "No. Oh no! Both of them?"

He didn't answer. He didn't have to.

"What about Logan and Maddy?"

"That's what took me so long. I wanted to make sure they weren't alone somewhere."

"Did you find them?"

His eyes lost focus, the image in his mind troubling him. "Yeah."

I took in a staggered breath and covered my face. I sat down hard onto a chair next to the kitchen table.

"What?" Halle said, not understanding.

I shook my head, got myself together, and wiped my eyes before smiling at Halle.

"I'm just glad they got to where they were going," I said, turning to walk over to the stove. I stirred the ravioli in the pot, forcing the sadness away.

Dad walked up behind me and kissed the crown of my head. "You can give your mom the note yourself."

I nodded.

"I found the keys to a Taurus with gas, but it had a bad alternator. I'll look again tomorrow. I'm going to put up these boards this afternoon. I need you to watch my back."

"Okay," I said, pulling the pot from the stove.

Dad washed his hands and face. Then, he took one of the bowls I'd poured the ravioli into and set it on the table in front of Halle. "I have something else for you, Pop Can."

"What?" she asked, turning to look up at him.

He held a pair of white Skechers in front of him. They were slip-ons with bungee-cord laces.

Halle gasped and used her toes to kick off her shoes. Then, she pulled the Skechers onto her feet. She walked toward the living room and then back. "They fit!"

I clapped and gave Dad a high five. "Yay!"

Dad went back to the kitchen for our bowls of ravioli, and after I took my bowl from him, we each sat down on an end of the table.

"I found out what the smoke was from," Dad said. "The gas station is in ashes. Looks like someone hit it with a car. That explains the huge explosion."

"Man. Bad way to go out," I said, chewing.

"A lot of the infected are charred, too. That's what the smell is from."

"You called it," I said.

"But the silver lining is, you can smell them coming, even more than usual."

"This is nice," Halle said, kicking her feet back and forth and chewing with her mouth open. "All we need is Mom."

Dad and I craned our necks in Halle's direction.

"What?" she asked.

Dad spent the next day looking for keys to cars with gas, and Halle and I played hide-and-seek in the big house with promises not to scream when one of us found the other.

I caught the man making another trip to the red brick house again, and he brought out more guns. For the last week, he'd done this every day around mid-morning, and then he'd stopped. I was beginning to wonder how many guns were in that house. From my reports, Dad had learned when not to be on our road, so he wouldn't cross paths with a man who obviously had a lot of firepower.

A few days after the man had stopped making trips to the brick house, I saw him again. This time, he was heading north. When the gunfire began, I panicked, worrying that Dad had run into him, but Dad returned quickly after, worried that it was Halle and me who had had the run-in.

After that, I would watch the man walk north every day. The sporadic gunfire would go on for an hour or two, and then shortly after, he would return home. It didn't take long for me to figure out what he was doing. He was slowly clearing the infected from the town, but I still didn't trust him enough to introduce myself.

A week had gone by, and I vowed to be patient.

Halfway through week two, that patience was waning.

At the end of week three, I began to feel resentful. Dad had stopped going out every day, and even though I tried really hard to trust him, he hadn't talked about a plan in quite a while.

One evening after dinner, I saw a group walking down the road. My eyes bulged. It was three men and a woman. They looked like they'd been on the road for a while.

"Dad!" I called as quietly as I could to the lower level. "Dad!"

"What?" he said, quickly climbing up. He looked out the window and then pushed me to the side, out of sight. "Who are they?" he asked, his back to the wall.

He was turned just right to keep an eye on them, and I mimicked his stance.

My eyebrows pulled together. "Why are you asking me?"

Dad shrugged. "Because you called me up here."

"Because there are people, new ones. That's worth mentioning, isn't it?"

We watched them while they hacked and stabbed at the infected. They seemed pretty adept, and I felt strangely drawn to them. The men were all dark-haired—one, tall and buff; one, very tall; and the other, short but clearly athletic. The woman was slender, her face hidden beneath a ball cap. Her hair was either very short or tucked up into the hat. The only way I could tell it was a woman was by her prominent…chest. She must have been tough to run with those three guys. One of the taller ones looked like a serial killer—albeit, a cute one. He reminded me of that actor who always played a soldier in movies.

"It's dark. They'd better find some shelter," Dad said.

"I think that's what they're doing. Oh no."

"What?" he said, leaning against the window to get a better look.

"They're going into the neighbor's house. He's home."

"Well, if we hear gunshots, we'll know they didn't get along."

The streetlights went out—all of them.

Dad went into the bathroom and flipped the switch. *Nothing.* He scrambled to the bathtub and began filling it with water.

I walked over to the doorway, staring at him. "What are you doing?"

"Go downstairs and do the same. When the electricity goes, so does the water! Go!"

I did as he'd commanded. I rushed down the stairs to the other bathroom and turned the tub faucet, opening it all the way.

After his tub was full, Dad ambled downstairs. "Well, that's it, I guess. Easy days are over."

"It's been easy? I think I'll go kill myself now."

Dad scowled. "Not funny."

"Sorry," I said. "You didn't really let us use the electricity anyway."

"The fridge," he grumbled.

"Oh, yeah." I sulked.

Halle called to Dad from the bed, and we blew out the candles and walked upstairs together. He went to bed, and I stood at the window, waiting for gunshots that never happened.

I couldn't shake the feeling that the group we had seen meant protection. I wanted to call out to them, be with them. Something about them felt safe.

I walked away from the window, wondering what was going on inside the neighbor's house, and I crawled into bed next to Halle. I worried about waking up to company of the uninfected variety, but at the same time, I hoped we would.

In the morning, I scrambled from bed so quickly that Dad jumped up in a panic.

"What?" he said, blinking.

I stood at the window, looking for any signs of the group. If they had decided to move on from Shallot, I assumed they would start at first light, and I was right. The men and woman had already passed our house, and they were walking along our street toward the highway, fearlessly taking down any infected that came within ten feet. But this time, the neighbor was with them.

"They know each other," Dad said from behind me. "Maybe he's been waiting for them this whole time."

"Or maybe they just met last night, and he's leaving with them because they're from someplace better?" I said.

"Maybe they're leading him to his death?"

I wrinkled my nose. "That doesn't make any sense. You're paranoid."

"Ya think?"

I turned to him. "When are *we* leaving?"

"I'm working on it," Dad said.

"What does that mean?" I asked.

Dad retreated to the bathroom, rubbing the back of his neck. He always did that when he and Mom fought, especially when she was making points he didn't have a rebuttal to.

I breathed out in frustration, shaking my head. He couldn't stay in the bathroom forever. I checked on Halle, and upon seeing her still sleeping deeply, I walked downstairs, lighting the candles in the kitchen and living room.

When Dad finally came down, I didn't waste any time.

"Have you thought about it?"

"Jenna," he said with a sigh, "don't rush me."

"Rush? We've been here for weeks. Are you at least going to go out today?"

"I'm going to check out the neighbor's house and see if he left anything behind."

"What does it matter if we're leaving?"

"Just because the neighbor left doesn't mean we have to."

"I don't want to leave because the neighbor did. I want to see my mom!"

Halle plodded down the stairs. "Why are you yelling?" she croaked.

"We're not," Dad said. "What do you want for breakfast? Pop-Tarts?"

"Sure," Halle said, sitting at the table.

I stomped into the nearly empty pantry and then tossed the box onto the table. The last five silver packages spilled out, some falling to the floor.

"Jenna!" Dad leaned back and then forward to clean the mess. "What's gotten into you?"

"My birthday is coming up. You promised."

"I know, and I said, I'm working on it."

"Working on what? You haven't left the house in days! We're running out of food!"

"Jenna," Dad said, glancing at Halle, "I haven't found a car. I'm...prolonging the inevitable."

"Which is what?" I asked, crossing my arms.

"I can't leave you alone. What if something happens while I'm gone?"

"Then, let's *go*!" I insisted.

"I've been..." He trailed off, already regretting his next words. "I've been wandering out that way, going a little bit farther every day. A lot of infected are on the roads, Jenna, and not just that. They're in the fields, and..."

"And what?"

"When I got to the white tower you girls have talked about, they're everywhere. Dead. I mean, *dead*, dead. It got worse the farther I walked. Something's going on over there, and I don't like it."

I snorted. "You're worried about dead infected? Isn't that a good thing?"

"That group has me nervous."

"That's *stupid*. Why don't we just start walking? The neighbor left with that group, and he's been smart about things. What if they're from Red Hill?"

"I have a bad feeling, Jenna! Something's off! I've felt this way for the past two weeks, like something bad is getting ready to happen."

"It's because my birthday is coming up, and you know that's your deadline. You're comfortable. You're complacent! But I'm not letting Mom think that we're dead one more day because you have a bad feeling!"

"Okay! All right!" he said, holding up his hands. "We'll leave in the morning."

"Really?" I said, perking up.

"Really. But if anything happens, no matter how far we are, we're coming straight back here. Do you understand?"

I agreed, and Halle did, too.

"And…we need to talk about…we need to talk about what to do and where to go if she's not there."

I sat back in my chair, feeling like I'd been gut-punched. "She's there," I said. "She's waiting for us, and you're going to feel like a huge jerk for even putting that awful thought in our heads."

"I hope so," Dad said. "I've never wanted to feel like a jerk more in my entire life."

chapter seventeen

THE SUN HAD JUST PEEKED OUT from the horizon when we stepped into the backyard. Halle and I had taken extra steps to look nice for Mom. I'd braided her hair, and she'd tucked in her shirt.

"Mom will get to see my new shoes!" she said with a wide grin and bright eyes.

It was the happiest I'd seen her in a long time.

"That's right. For now, let's stay focused and keep an eye out. Remember what Dad said about lots of weird stuff on the roads. Listen, and pay attention to your surroundings."

Halle emphatically bobbed her head.

I had helped her slip on her backpack, and I had tied her jacket around her waist before we left the house. Her head seemed bare, and I realized her hat was still in my hand.

"Don't forget this," I said, handing it to her.

Dad was quiet, but I didn't want to talk to him about it. I was afraid he'd change his mind.

We walked down the back alley as the birds and crickets chirped. The gravel crunched beneath our feet, and Dad's pants made that familiar swishing noise that I only noticed when we were on foot.

Dad had been forced to tighten his belt two notches since all this had started, and his pants sagged in the backside. I didn't make a habit of looking in the mirror, but it wasn't hard to see that we had all lost weight. The more I thought about it, the more I prepared myself that Mom would look different, too.

My heart leaped. We would know by the end of the day. I was just as excited to calm her fears as I was to see her.

When we stepped out from behind Shallot's hill onto Highway 123 and turned north, that was when I really began to get excited. Seeing Mom today was actually happening. Dad was still quiet, twisting the wooden handle of the trident he'd found in someone's barn the week before. He still carried the semiautomatic rifle he'd found on the overpass near Anderson, and I still carried his rifle and Jud's aluminum bat, but because of the man with the guns, it was easier to get out of town than it was to get in.

I never found out if the man—whoever he was—was trustworthy, but he was definitely smart. Walking to that side of town every day to shoot the infected had not only thinned out the undead population, but the noise had also drawn them to the opposite side of town from where we'd stayed. When we'd left, we'd only come across a handful.

Dad was right. We hadn't been on the road for more than twenty minutes when we discovered the first group. They were headed north, but we were upwind. Once we got close enough, they turned toward our smell.

"Get ready," Dad said. "Knees first and then the head. Swing hard. Halle?"

"Yeah?" she said, fear nearly drowning out her voice.

"Stay out of the way, but don't just focus on us. Pay attention to your surroundings."

When the first infected got close enough to Dad, he thrust the trident into its face. It immediately froze, and when Dad jerked out the metal prongs, it fell to the ground. He went for another one, and I twisted the grip of the bat, holding it low and to the side, until I was close enough. They were mostly focused on Dad. It seemed like whenever one was killed, those around it became agitated and more fixated on the aggressor.

I swung at the knees of a woman approaching Dad's side, and then I swung again when she fell to the ground.

"Get back a little, Jenna. Stay close to Halle!"

I complied and fell back, glancing behind me. Halle was standing in the middle of the road, like Dad had instructed the night before. She was watching us but also looking around herself often.

"You're doing good, Halle. Keep it up!" I said, swinging at an infected that came too close.

Within minutes, the group was down, and Dad and I were standing over them, breathing hard and smiling.

"We did it," I said, huffing.

"Good job, kiddo," Dad said. "You all right, Halle?"

She ran to my side, hugging my arm. "Let's hurry!"

We continued walking in a slower pace until we caught our breaths, and then Dad set it a bit faster.

"You made me proud back there."

"Yeah?" I said.

He grabbed the bill of my hat and playfully pulled it down. "Yeah. We make a good team."

"Told you so," I said with a smug smile.

"You, too," he said to Halle.

She looked up, squinting one eye, and grinned.

"You're different," I said. "In a good way. You don't really yell anymore, and you don't get super mad."

Dad hooked his arm around my neck. "Well, maybe the apocalypse forced me to grow up."

"I think Mom will be surprised."

"You think so?" He chuckled.

"Yeah, and she'll be grateful to you for bringing us safely to her, for taking care of us all this time."

"Well, that's nice, but…I didn't do it for her. I did it because you're my kids, and I love you."

Halle hugged one side of him, and I hugged the other. We stood there together in the middle of the road in a tangled wad of love, acceptance, and gratitude. I felt like Dad and I finally had an understanding, and I knew that things would be different once we got to the ranch—between him and Mom, too.

As the sun rose and the heat turned everything a foot off the highway into wavy lines, our lovefest turned into a single line of sweat and determination. We weren't halfway there, and Halle needed shade and a water break.

Dad took a sip from his canteen and handed it to me. "We're going to have to step it up, girls. At this pace, we won't make it by nightfall."

I looked to my baby sister. "I know it's hot but think about Mom. Just keep thinking about Mom."

"Don't let the heat keep you from paying attention to your surroundings," Dad said. "We have to—"

Too late, I heard the moan. After all the infected we had slipped by and taken down, it just took one to appear from the trees and sink his teeth into Dad's forearm.

Dad cried out and pulled the creature down with him.

Halle screamed, too, but I didn't have the luxury of being afraid or even being sad. I was angry. Dad had been bitten, and I could see in his eyes, and he in mine, that it was over. A few miles ago, we had just come to an understanding. We had just figured everything out. Things were going to be different. I funneled every bit of that anger into my bat, and with one swing, the infected went from gnawing on Dad's arm to a lifeless, harmless body on the ground.

Halle was still screaming when Dad stood. She was staring at his arm like it was on fire.

"I'm sorry," I said, my voice thick with emotion and my chest heaving. "I'm so sorry."

"The first-aid kit!" he said, pointing to his pack.

He turned around, and I pulled on the zipper, lifting out the plastic container.

"What? What do I do?" I asked. The tears were falling then.

Halle's screams blurred in the background.

"The tourniquet!"

I handed him the stretchy band.

"The gauze and the tape!"

After he tied the tourniquet with his good hand and his teeth, he placed one large square of gauze on the wound and then another before wrapping the tape around his arm on each end.

I held out a can of antibiotic spray. "Do you need this before you tape it?" I asked.

"It won't do any good." He looked at Halle and me, hopelessness in his eyes. "I'm so sorry, girls." His eyes filled with tears. "I'm so, so sorry."

We hugged Dad again—this time, with no understanding and no peace. We were all sobbing.

Dad sat down and leaned back against a tree. "I'm going to rest for five minutes."

"Halle, give him the water," I said.

The anger had gone away, leaving only an empty ache mixed with fear. I thought about how Tavia had leaned over her brother's body and how that scene hadn't been anything like what I was feeling. I thought about Connor and how he existed every day with emptiness in his eyes. I always believed he was just suffering unbearable sadness that he couldn't describe with words, but sad was wrong. *Sad* was a common term, and this was very specific. It was unique only to those who had been unlucky enough to experience it, yet it was different for everyone. Dad would run into burning buildings for a living. He would bring people back to life. He was invincible. But there he sat, next to a tree, mentally preparing to die, to leave his young daughters alone. He didn't say it, but I could see the torture within him, swirling in his eyes.

"We'd better go," he said. I reached to help him to his feet. "I don't know how long I have."

"Back to Shallot?" I asked.

"I'm sorry, Jenna. I really am," he said, his voice breaking.

"Whatever you want to do. Let's just get you somewhere to rest," I said.

"C'mon, Pop Can," Dad said, reaching out for Halle.

My bottom lip quivered, and I supported his every step, slow but steady, all the way back to where we'd started. With each step, the guilt bore down on me. It was heavier than Dad. He'd had a bad feeling. It wasn't because of a deadline or even that Mom wasn't going to be there when we arrived. He'd felt his last day coming, and I'd pushed him into it.

Once in a while, he would groan at the pain in his arm, and it spread to his wrist and shoulder. Then, the headache began. By the time we got back to the dark green two-story house that had been our home for the past month, Dad was pale and soaked in sweat.

I helped him up the stairs of the back porch and into the living room where he collapsed onto the couch.

I looked at Halle. "I'm going to check the house first. You stay here."

Checking each room, behind every door and inside every closet, I made certain the house was clear, and the windows were still secure. I couldn't take care of Dad and worry about what might sneak up on us.

I ran into the bathroom and put water onto a washcloth. I tried not to cry, whispering to myself to be strong. He was going to die, but I could make it easier on everyone if I kept it together. I looked up at the dusty mirror. My hairline was wet with sweat, my face pink from the sun. My clothes were filthy, my eyes sunken and dim.

This was not like the video games. We didn't get to start over.

I went into the living room. I knelt next to the couch and propped Dad's head with a pillow. He sucked in air through his teeth, making a hissing noise.

"Everything hurts?" I asked.

"Like the worst flu in the history of ever," he said with a weak smile.

I wiped his face with the rag and then folded it before gently laying it across his forehead. "This is bad," I whispered in a brittle small voice. "I don't know what to do."

"Yes, you do. Jenna, listen to me. We've planned for this. I had the flu shot. I'm going to go downhill fast." His stomach and chest heaved once, and then he swallowed.

"Go get a bowl," I said to Halle.

"But——" she began.

"Now!"

"Jenna," Dad said, "keep the gun on you until I quit breathing."

I shook my head. "I don't wanna do this. Please don't make me."

"Don't wait. Don't even say good-bye. Have Halle go into the other room, and take care of it."

I pursed my lips, trying to hold in the sob. My vision blurred with tears. I was going to have to shoot my dad. What kind of world was this? Nothing could have prepared me for this conversation and definitely not for the act itself.

"Daddy…"

He furrowed his brow and pulled me against his chest. "I'm sorry you have to do this," he said, his voice breaking. "I love you so much."

"I love you, too," I said through faltering breath. "I love you, too."

He let me go. "Promise me, you'll take care of your sister, no matter what."

"I promise," I said, wiping his face again.

Halle returned with a large bowl, her cheeks wet and red. When she saw my expression, her lip jutted out and trembled.

He pulled his mouth to the side, regret in his eyes. "Jenna, you're smart. You're smarter than me, and it's going to save you and your sister more than once. Trust your instincts. Use your head, not your heart." He grabbed the bowl and heaved into it, expelling the contents of his stomach, which wasn't much. He leaned back against the couch, his face a sallow color. The veins beneath his skin were beginning to darken.

"I don't want you to die, Daddy," Halle said, sucking in breaths.

He pulled her in. "It's going to be okay, Pop Can. You're going to be okay. You're so strong. You're both so strong. I trust your sister to take care of you. You have to trust her, too."

"Okay," she said, sniffing and nodding against his chest. He let her go, she pushed her glasses up the bridge of her nose. "I want you to be okay though. Please be okay."

Dad's bottom lip pulled up. "I can't. I wish I could. I'm sorry." He swallowed and then vomited again.

It was happening fast. I had the strangest sensation come over me. I didn't want him to leave us, but I was desperate for his suffering to end.

"Don't get in a hurry to leave," Dad said. "Don't make emotional decisions. Think about things first—for several days, if you have to. When you think you have it all figured out, think on it some more. And get a good feel for the neighbor before you talk to him. Take a gun, but don't let him know you have one. Teach Halle how to protect herself." He looked up. "I'm forgetting something. I need to tell you everything. I should have taught you how to drive a car, how to—" His stomach lurched, and he groaned as he threw up into the bowl again.

I leaned back and looked up at the ceiling.

"I was so worried about protecting you that I forgot to teach you how to survive without me."

"You did good, Dad. We're going to be okay."

I stood and took the bowl to the toilet. I emptied it and then rinsed it out in the sink before returning quickly to Dad's side. He was so hot that I could feel the fever radiating off his skin. His eyes were bloodshot, and his veins kept getting darker as the virus took hold of his body.

"You will because you're tough like your mom. You can do this."

"Halle," I said, "get another wet rag for his head."

She obeyed without question.

After an hour, he seemed to stop fighting, and his body relaxed. He was exhausted. He could barely move. Halle was sitting in the recliner across the room, staring at him. I was trying my best to keep him comfortable—changing out the rags for his head and his arm and giving him water even though it would come right back up.

I wanted to beg him not to do this, not to make me do this, but he had no choice, and neither did I. We both had to be strong for Halle until the end, and I had to be strong after. I tried not to let my mind wander to thoughts of what it would be like to survive alone with my sister. We had to survive his death first.

"Jenna," he drawled.

A thick mucus had formed in the corners of his mouth. His veins had branched out under his graying skin, dark and frightening—like the monster he would become. I'd seen those things so many times, but none of them looked like someone I knew. None of them looked like anyone I loved.

"Yes, Daddy?"

"I love you. I love Halle. Get ready."

He sucked in a few more shallow breaths and then paused for a moment. Then, he exhaled it all, never taking in another breath. His head fell to the side, and his eyes stared past me, vacant.

I choked back a cry. "Dad?" I swallowed. "Daddy?"

His words about not waiting repeated in my mind, and I nudged him.

Nothing.

I put my hand over his eyes to close them, and then I stood. "Halle, go into the other room and cover your ears."

I pulled the thick black strap from my shoulder and held the rifle in both hands, steadying my feet.

"Daddy!" Halle cried, reaching for him.

I stopped her with one hand, holding her away. "Go into the other room, so I can do this before he turns."

"Jenna, don't!" she yelled.

"I don't want to! I have to!" I said, twin waterfalls spilling down my cheeks. I checked the rifle's chamber and then took off the safety.

Dad's fingers twitched.

"Jenna, look! He's still alive!" Halle cried. "Don't do it!"

His lids opened to reveal two milky eyes, and then he blinked. He looked over at me, and his lips began to form a snarl.

My chest lurched as I held back a sob. "Please look away, Halle." I raised the rifle, and through the tears streaming from my eyes, I aimed and pulled the trigger.

chapter eighteen

HALLE PLAYED WITH A PORCELAIN CAT and a coffee mug in the shape of a chicken next to the kitchen table as I tried to keep busy. We'd eaten the last of the rice for dinner the night before, and Halle had become nearly hysterical at the thought of me leaving her to find food.

She played with her toys while her stomach growled.

"We have to get food somehow," I said.

"Then, let me go with you," she said.

I sighed.

She stood up and walked the edge of the living room to get to the bathroom for a drink of water. She wouldn't go all the way into the living room anymore. I didn't really like to either. I couldn't get the bloodstains off the couch, so I'd covered it with a bedsheet, which wasn't much better.

Halle stopped wanting to go outside, not that it was safe anyway. I wasn't sure if it was because the neighbor had stopped drawing the infected to the other side of town with his gunshots, but there seemed to be more of them roaming the streets and yards. Though, many of them were wandering out of town toward the highway.

I felt bad for Halle, not being able to play under the shade trees in the yard, especially since it was so hot inside. We'd open the windows upstairs in the evenings just to keep it comfortable enough to sleep. Every day that went by, the sadder she became, and the less she ate. She wouldn't even look out the back door to the yard, not wanting to see the shallow grave where we had buried our dad.

I'd hold her at night while she cried herself to sleep, wishing I had the luxury of doing that, too. I pretended to be the adult though because that was what my sister needed.

I wondered if Halle and I should just stay or if we should chance the road to Red Hill ranch. Now that there were so many infected, it seemed impossible even if we wanted to.

We had done the opposite of what Dad had always taught us to do—pay attention to our surroundings. We had been lulled into a false sense of safety in the shade of trees and off the road. That one mistake had led to Dad's death. I was trying to decide if it was more important to keep Halle alive here in Shallot—at least until she was old enough to travel—or attempt the daylong walk to the ranch without making a single mistake, so we could be with our mom.

Dad had been faced with that same choice, and I'd rushed him even though he asked me not to. Knowing the result of that hasty decision made it easier to ignore my emotions urging me to leave for Red Hill and to spend more time thinking about a strategy. There were only two of us now, and Halle wasn't strong enough to fight off the infected. I couldn't take on more than one, maybe two, and we had come across more groups than we had loners.

Unless it rained soon, I wasn't sure how much longer the water would last even if we stopped using it for anything but drinking. Leaving Halle alone to go scavenging was the most terrifying thing. If something happened to me, she would have no one. It wasn't impossible, but the odds of her surviving alone were low, and I had promised Dad that I'd take care of her. I couldn't take care of her if I were dead.

It had been at least a week since we lost Dad. The days were blurring together. My birthday was coming up, give or take a few days. It had been months since the first day of the outbreak. Mom probably thought we were dead, and I wanted so much to prove to her that she was wrong. But I couldn't think about that anymore. I had to concentrate on Halle.

"Halle, if the neighbor comes back, I'm going to go out and talk to him."

"What?" she said, frozen.

"I want you to bring Dad's knife. If he tries to grab me and I can't get away, you're going to have to help."

"You mean, stab him?"

"Yes."

"Okay."

Her answer surprised me. I knew that Dad's death had changed her, but she was no longer the whiny, needy little girl that she used to be. She listened to me the way that she used to listen to our parents—without argument. She trusted me.

"Okay," I said.

I heard a moan outside, and instinctively, Halle blew out the candle and rushed over to me. We hunkered down together beneath the window, and I wrapped my arms tightly around her.

"Whoa! Watch out!" a man yelled from the street.

Halle looked up at me. "The neighbor?" she whispered.

I held my finger over my mouth, listening to the exchange outside. It was dark, and we couldn't be sure who was outside.

"There are even more than last time! It's too dark! Let's go! Let's go!"

"Skeeter! Your eleven o'clock!" Two gunshots popped. "I'll lead them away from the house and meet you there!"

Skeeter? The guy from Fairview who saved Connor? My heart boomed in my chest. *Skeeter could be trusted. Skeeter would help us.*

"Joey, come on!"

"I'll be there in a second! Go!"

There was another moan, and this time, it was right outside the window. After a scuffle and a loud crack, I heard more moaning, and then the back door opened and closed.

Halle stiffened.

A man stood in the living room with a baseball bat in his hand. He was breathing hard, drenched in sweat, splattered in dark blood, and staring down at us in shock.

"Hi," he said.

Halle looked up at me and then back to the man. He had been with the group before, the one who had taken our neighbor. He was the big, tall one, the one who looked like the beautiful serial killer.

I leaned over to retrieve Dad's rifle, and I pointed it at him.

He held up his hands. "Whoa, whoa! I'm not going to hurt you. Just trying to get away from the teds out there."

"What are teds?" Halle asked.

I shushed her.

He took a step, his hands still in the air. "Are your parents here?"

"Where's Skeeter?" I asked.

His eyebrows lifted. "You know Skeeter?"

"Where is he?" I asked.

"He's with our group a few houses down." He stared at Halle for a moment and then at me.

I moved to my knees, slowly pushing Halle behind me. "Don't come any closer."

"Okay. Would it make you feel better if I gave you my stuff and sat down?"

"Your weapons?" I asked.

He nodded once.

"Slowly," I said in a firm voice. "Slide them this way."

He rolled his bat over to us, and then he pulled a 9mm from behind him, holding it by the grip. He slid that over as well. "I have a knife in my boot. Do you want that?"

"Just keep your hands away from your shoes," I said.

He lowered himself, moving slowly, until both knees were on the ground like mine. He placed his hands on his thighs, palms down. "Are you from Fairview, too?" he asked.

I stood, still pointing the gun at his face. "No," I said, refusing to let my guard down. "Who else is in your group? Where are you from?"

"We're staying in a farmhouse northeast of here. We have some kids there. One's about her age," he said, nodding to Halle.

"Don't look at her," I said. "Look at me."

He blinked, surprised at my relentless suspicion.

"I'm really not going to hurt you. I can leave if you want, but…if you're alone, I can't really leave you here."

I narrowed my eyes at him. "Why do you keep trying to find out if we're alone?"

He held up his hands. "Listen, we got off on the wrong foot. My name is Joey. We're not criminals or anything. We've been clearing the road between here and our place for our friend. She's got two daughters coming and…" His eyes danced between us. "No way. Oh my *God*. You're not…"

I pulled my eyebrows together, watching him closely.

"Are you Scarlet's girls?" he said, his eyes wide.

"Jenna!" Halle said.

Joey laughed once and covered his mouth. "Holy shit, you're Jenna and Halle! Your mom is right down the street!"

"What?" I said, my eyes instantly tearing.

"Mommy!" Halle said, standing.

I gathered my composure and pushed Halle back behind me, repositioning my gun.

Joey held his hands higher. "I swear. We've been coming this way almost every day, helping her clear the teds to make it safer for you girls to get to Red Hill. Where's your dad? Andrew?"

Once he said Dad's name, I relaxed, and my gun pointed toward the floor. Halle threw her arms around my butt in excitement. I breathed out and began to sob uncontrollably.

"It's okay, Jenna. Mom is just down the street!"

"It's…it's okay," Joey said. "Can I…can I hug you?"

I didn't respond. All I could do was bawl. So much relief and happiness came over me, two emotions I hadn't felt in a very long time. It was too overwhelming.

Joey approached us slowly. He took the gun from my hands, clicked the safety, and then put it on the floor nearby before gently wrapping his large arms around Halle and me. My knees gave way, but he effortlessly bore my weight.

"Okay," he said in a comforting tone, "we're going to get you to your mom. She is going to…I don't even know. I can't wait to see her smile."

That thought helped dry my tears, and I looked down to Halle. "Get your things. We're going to see Mom."

Halle ran to fetch her backpack, and I grabbed mine before slinging the rifle over my shoulder.

Joey picked up his weapons, shaking his head. "I can't believe I found you. I can't believe you're both alive."

"Does she think we're dead?"

"Nope. She's been watching the hill for you every day. She never gave up."

For the first time since the morning we'd left for Red Hill with Dad, I was filled with hope.

"Here, let me carry those," he said, taking our packs. "It's dark, so listen for anything shuffling around. Stay close."

"Okay," we said in unison.

This is really happening. Mom is just a couple of minutes away.

Joey stepped out of the back door, and I began to follow him, but then the door slammed in my face.

Joey turned to face us while an infected sank its teeth into his neck.

"No," I said, looking into his wide eyes while flattening my palms against the Plexiglas. "No!"

"Stay inside," he whispered before pushing backward and then stumbling away. Several infected followed him, and then he disappeared into the darkness.

Halle took a breath and began to scream, but I covered her mouth and pulled her to the floor. I reached up and turned the lock, and then I rocked her while we listened to the crickets and the excited moans of infected shuffling through the yard after Joey.

I concentrated on my breathing, trying to slow it down. My eyes began to get fuzzy, and my nose felt numb.

I held my breath for a moment, and then I took in a shallow breath through my nostrils before blowing it out. The next one was more controlled. After several more of those, I felt better.

I realized I was still rocking Halle, my hand covering her mouth. I quickly pulled my hand away, and she wiped her eyes.

"Are we still going to see Mom?" she whispered.

"It's too risky. We'll catch her in the morning before she leaves town."

"He has my backpack," Halle said, her bottom lip quivering.

"I'll find you a new one."

I pulled a dresser in front of the bottom of the stairs and set drinking glasses and vases on top, just like we had done our first night. Then, I did the same at the top of the stairs.

Halle and I didn't attempt to sponge bathe like usual. We just went straight to bed. I knew that no matter what happened, the next day would be a long one.

"I want Mom," Halle whimpered.

"Me, too. We're going to see her tomorrow."

"You keep saying that, but we never do."

"I promise, Halle. One way or another, we will see Mom tomorrow."

"Okay," she said.

It took Halle longer than usual to fall asleep, and then she jerked and muttered and cried in her sleep, likely dreaming about Joey or Dad.

The moaning outside continued for hours, and I wondered if I was ever going to fall asleep. The heat didn't help, and neither did thinking every noise was an infected trying to get into the house or thinking about seeing Mom the next day.

I thought about the first time I had seen the group, and I wondered if the woman I had seen was Mom.

Did she look so different that I wouldn't recognize her? Would she recognize us? Would she think we had changed? Had she?

I thought about Connor and how different he was from the boy April had described and how quickly he had changed. We had been apart from Mom for months, and by Joey's description, she was now in the business of killing zombies so that we could get to Red Hill. I imagined what she was like now. It didn't matter how much she'd changed though. With her was the only place I wanted to be, and it was worth anything to get there.

My eyes finally began to feel heavy, and I let it take me away from Shallot to the halls of Bishop Middle School.

I walked and talked with Chloe, confused about where my classes were, and I was frustrated because I couldn't remember my locker combination.

Chloe shook her head and frowned at me. "Jenna?"

"Yeah?"

"Wake up."

I opened my eyes to see Halle leaning over me, pushing up her black-rimmed glasses. "Jenna? Are we seeing Mom today?"

I pushed her to the side and sat up, seeing the bright sun shining through the windows. "No. No!" I said, running to the window at the top of the stairs.

They would have left at first light. I'd overslept. I'd missed them.

"Fill the canteen with water, Halle!" I said, pushing the dresser out of the way. "We're leaving!"

I stuffed the last slices of beef jerky into my back pocket. I grabbed the rifle, the last box of ammo, and then a sack full of newspapers with a box of matches.

"Get the bat and Dad's hunting knife," I said.

"What are you doing with that?" Halle asked, pointing to the matches.

I looked outside, seeing several infected in the backyard. The street had several, but there weren't so many that we couldn't outrun them.

"We're going out the front door."

"Why?" she asked. We'd never done that before because there were often infected in the street.

I dumped the bag of papers onto the couch and pushed it against the wall, draping the curtains over the cushions. I lit several matches, held them under a few newspapers, and then watched as it turned into flames. The other papers caught, and I tossed some of the bullets into the fire.

"What are you doing?" Halle cried.

"Creating a diversion," I said, watching as the flames climbed the curtains.

The room quickly began to fill with smoke, so I opened the front door and pulled Halle through.

We ran out into the street, straight into a group of infected.

We ran the other way, stopped by several more.

"Jenna," Halle said, afraid.

Smoke billowed from the front door, and then one of the plywood sheets broke open with a snap. The infected turned toward the house, but when I pulled Halle along, they began to follow.

Then, the bullets began to pop and crack, gaining the full attention of the creatures. I tugged on Halle's hand, and we sprinted for the highway, finally passing the car sitting in the middle of the road. I only slowed down when Halle began to fall behind.

We stopped for a moment, both grabbing our knees and heaving, until we caught our breaths. The sun was bearing down on us, and only then did I realize I hadn't grabbed a hat or sunscreen for Halle.

"I'm sorry," I said, knowing Halle's pained expression matched mine. "We have to hurry if we're going to get to Red Hill before dark."

"Where's Mom?"

"She's probably almost there by now."

"When will we get there?"

"Before dark, if we're lucky."

I took the first step, and Halle followed.

We held hands, the summer sun merciless, the road sending sizzling heat up our legs. My pants were an inch shorter than they had been in the spring, and Halle's were, too. The cicadas hissed in the grass as we passed by.

Every fifteen minutes or so, I would initiate a jog but only for as long as Halle could go.

"It's too hot to run," Halle said.

"But if we don't once in a while, we won't make it before dark."

"I'm thirsty," she said.

I pulled the canteen strap from around my neck and handed it to her. She took a big sip.

"Easy, Pop Can. That has to last us all day."

"Sorry," she said, handing it back. "Jenna?"

"Yeah?"

"Please don't call me that. It makes me miss Dad."

"Sorry," I said.

I could see a small group of infected ahead, and I quietly alerted Halle. It wasn't safe to travel too far into the wheat field, but I decided it was better than trying to run around them.

"Listen to the wheat," I said. "You can hear them coming."

Halle nodded, and we ducked into the tall stalks. Leaning down, we tiptoed past the half-dozen infected. There were a few children with them, and it made me feel nauseous.

That isn't going to happen to us, not before we see our mom.

After we were several blocks ahead of the group, we leaped out of the stalks and kept a quick pace until they were so far behind that we couldn't see them.

"Look," Halle said, pointing to the pillar of smoke in the air. "That's our house."

"No going back now even if we wanted to."

"I don't want to anyway," Halle said.

"If something happens to me, you keep going," I said.

"Jenna—"

"I'm serious, Halle. Keep being sneaky until you get there. You know the way. Just keep walking, keep listening, and pay attention to your surroundings. You'll get there."

Halle screamed, and we stumbled back. A large infected stumbled out from the wheat field in front of us and then another.

"Stay away!" I called to Halle. "Keep an eye out!"

She had the bat, so I used the stock of my gun to wipe out the infected's knees. Then, I took out the large knife tucked in the back of my pants and thrust downward into its eye. His arms and legs went limp. Then, I swung the rifle high before hitting the second one in the head with a *thwack*. She toppled backward, and then I hit her a second time. She didn't move, but I was only holding the barrel of the rifle in my hand. It had broken in half when I hit her.

"No!" I said, looking at the useless metal in my hand. I tossed it to the ground and kicked at it. "Crap!" I yelled.

Halle shushed me. "You can't fix it?" she asked.

I shook my head.

"Let's go." I took her hand, and we continued on the asphalt.

It was miserably hot and sticky, and after a while, we quit holding hands because the sweat made them slip away anyway.

Every five minutes or so, I had to encourage Halle to keep up. Every mile we gained, the more decomposed bodies were piled on each side of the road. I could tell they'd been dragged, and I knew it was Mom clearing the way for us, telling us to keep going.

"Halle," I said, breathless and exhausted, "look."

chapter nineteen

"THE WHITE TOWER!" Halle said, squinting one eye as she looked upward.

A tall white tube loomed above us, standing as a beacon for Red Hill. We left the highway for red dirt, and our pace naturally quickened.

"It's not far now!" I said, encouraging my sister. "Just a few more miles to the cemetery, and then we're practically there!"

We passed a large feedlot. I remembered hundreds, if not thousands, of cows milling about before, but now, there weren't any. We came across a large pile of dead infected and gave them a wide berth just in case.

After another hour of walking, I stopped and handed Halle the canteen. She took a large gulp and handed it to me. I did the same, and then I reached back for the beef jerky. It wasn't there. I turned around in a circle, as if it would appear if I could just see it.

"It must have fallen out when I scuffled with the infected."

Halle's shoulders sagged. "It's okay. Let's keep going."

"I'm so proud of you," I said to Halle.

"We're almost there, right? And Mom's there, right?" she said.

I could hear the exhaustion in her voice.

"Yes, and yes. I don't know how much farther, but I know we're going to get there before dark."

I hoped I was right. The sun was getting lower in the sky, and we had been walking for hours. We had to be close.

"Look!" Halle said, pointing ahead. "The cemetery!"

I grabbed her hand, and we ran toward it before turning left.

"Just a couple of more miles, Halle! We're almost there!"

"She is going to be so happy! Do you think she'll cry?"

"Yes. And I will, too."

Halle teared up, and so did I. Our hair was soaked in sweat, our lips were dry and chapped, our noses and foreheads were both bright pink from the sun, and I'd lost track of how many days it had been since we had a real shower. We weren't as pretty as we had wanted to be, but Mom wouldn't care.

"My side is hurting," Halle said.

"Want to get on my back?" I asked.

She shook her head. "No, it'll slow us down."

I smiled at her. She was so smart.

After another mile, we hit an intersection. To the right, about a hundred yards away, was a hill, and on the other side of that hill was the ranch. My stomach fluttered, and my heart began to pound. We were almost there.

"There's the hill," I said to Halle, pulling her to the west, toward the setting sun.

She dropped the bat as if she were letting go of all the bad things that had happened to us up to that point. "Good thing, too," she said. "It'll be dark soon."

I wanted to run, but I was just too tired, and I knew Halle was, too. So, we held hands as we approached the hill and climbed over. I looked at the farmhouse hoping to see Mom outside. Two people were sitting on the roof.

"I think that's Mom!" I said. "Look, Halle, on the roof!"

Two men ran out of the house. One climbed up a ladder to the roof, yelling, and the other waved his arms at us.

Halle and I began to run, and the woman on the roof shouted something in an excited, high-pitched voice.

"It's Mom!" I said, trying not to run ahead of Halle.

They began calling to us. Happy tears streamed down my face. I tightly gripped Halle's hand, worried I would get too excited and run too fast.

The men began to run toward us, and then a woman followed. Mom stayed on the roof and aimed the rifle she was holding.

Something is wrong.

Mom began to panic, shrieking words I couldn't understand. I slowed down, pulling Halle to a stop, and I looked around. The wheat was swishing. Mom could see something we couldn't. There were infected in the field. They were heading toward us.

"Run!" Mom screamed.

I looked behind me, tightened my grip on Halle's hand, and began sprinting toward the farmhouse. The men were running toward us, weapons in their hands. They must be friends of Mom's. They were just as invested as she was to get us to her, just like Joey had been.

The men called to us, motioning for us to run to them. I could run faster, but Halle's legs were going as fast as they could, and I wouldn't leave her behind.

Halle began to cry, the sound carrying every bit of her fear and relief, knowing that we were at the end of our journey either way.

A shot popped, echoing across the waving wheat. After a few seconds, I heard it again. It was Mom. She was shooting the infected in the field. The popping came steadily, each time cracking through the air, rumbling like thunder.

The first of the infected emerged from the wheat. I stopped and leaned back so hard that I fell, taking Halle with me.

The gunshots continued while I scrambled backward. A wall of tattered, rotting bodies formed between the men trying to save us and Halle and me. There were so many. It was as if the entire town of Shallot had followed us just to stop us right before we got to Mom.

The men and a woman began yelling to get the attention of the huge group of infected, but they kept coming at us. I could hear the wheat swishing behind us, and I knew we would be surrounded at any moment. I grabbed Halle and held her close.

"Mommy!" A shrill scream I barely recognized as my own emerged from my throat. "Mommy!"

A pop went off, and the closest infected fell, his brain matter spreading out and mixing with the red dirt. Another infected fell, and I knew Mom was taking out anything getting too close.

A man appeared from the field on the other side of the road and grabbed my arm. Halle and I screamed, but then the man pulled us up and pushed us behind him. Mom picked off another infected with her rifle, but there were more behind it. The man shoved one away from us, and it stumbled back, falling to the ground. Then, another shot went off, this one much closer.

Our neighbor was standing at the end of the gun that had gone off.

"Go, Nathan!" our neighbor said to the man holding my arm.

Nathan looked down at us. "We're going into the other field and around, okay? Follow me. Stay close!"

We ran into the tall stalks, hunkered down like before. Nathan stopped for a moment and listened, and then he pulled me as I dragged Halle along.

"Just a little bit farther," Nathan said, guiding us through the wheat.

We stepped out of the field and onto red dirt again. This time, we were right in front of the driveway. We crossed the road and went through the yard toward the porch. A woman with long blonde hair opened her arms wide and guided us into the house.

Halle reached behind her. "Mommy?"

The woman's eyes were wide and worried, but she offered a comforting smile. "She's just going to help the others. You're safe. You're safe."

Two other girls were inside, warily watching us. One was my age, and the other was closer to Halle's age.

More shots rang out over and over. Halle covered her ears, and I pulled her into me.

She shook her head, sobbing. "Where's Mommy?"

"She's right outside. She'll be here soon. Do you remember me, Halle? I'm Ashley, the doctor's daughter. We've met before."

Halle nodded and buried her face into my side. Now that we were here, the wait was agonizing.

After a few minutes, the crack of gunshots slowed down, and then they stopped altogether, both from the roof and the road.

"I think it's over," Ashley said. Then, her shoulders shot up to her ears when two more pops sounded.

Ashley rushed outside, and I followed.

There she was, our mother, standing on the front porch, seeing us but not truly believing. I collapsed into her arms, pressing my face into her chest. Only by hearing her cries did I know that Halle had done the same. We all fell together in a heap on the porch, and Mom's body began to tremble and then shake as she cried right along with us, like I knew she would.

Mom lifted my chin and then cupped my cheeks, looking into my eyes in awe. She looked down at Halle, too, and then we began to laugh before crying again.

Nathan and our neighbor guided the blonde back to the house. She was bawling hysterically, reaching for the road, until our neighbor finally resorted to forcing her inside. The walls barely muffled her wails.

Nathan watched Ashley and our neighbor until they disappeared behind the door, and then he looked down at us in awe. "You have some incredible kids there."

"Miranda?" Mom asked.

Nathan sighed. "Bryce was attacked. She tried to save him. I couldn't get to them in time."

Mom's shoulders fell, and then she kissed Halle's face, which was buried under my arm. Her dirty fingernails dug into my skin. I kissed her head.

"Come on, girls. I've got you. Let's go inside."

I hadn't heard Mom's voice in so long, but it was still as soft and strong as I remembered.

Nathan helped us up, and we walked inside together. Mom, Halle, and I kept looking at each other and smiling.

"We saw your message," I said, my voice breaking.

Mom shook her head in disbelief. "Where's your dad?"

"He was bit," Halle said in her small voice.

"He made us leave him," I said. "He made us."

I meant that he'd made me shoot him, but I couldn't say it out loud. Even if it had to be done, it sounded awful, and everyone in the room was listening.

"Shh...shh..." Mom said, hugging us. Her body slightly rocked, and I instantly felt at ease. "How long have you been alone?"

"I don't know," I said. "A week? I think."

"Wow," our neighbor said. "Tough like their mama."

I smiled and rested my cheek against Mom's chest. "That's what Dad said, too, when we left him. He said we could do it because we were tough like you."

Mom looked at Nathan, who was holding the other two little girls close. I could tell Mom was unhappy that we had been alone.

"If you hadn't cleared the way for them, it would have been tough for them to make it past Shallot alone, if not impossible," Nathan said. "You were right. It wasn't for nothing."

Her eyes glossed over, and she hugged us again.

I was wrong. She was more slender than I remembered, but she was still our mom. She hadn't changed so much. I hadn't realized how afraid I was that she wouldn't be the same person I knew. But now, in her arms, the past months fell away. It felt like a lifetime since she had dropped us off at school, but at the same time, it also felt like yesterday.

"Come on, babies. Let's get you cleaned up," Mom said. Halle whined, but Mom kissed her hair. "You're safe now." She looked to me. "When is the last time you've eaten? Or slept?"

My eyebrows pulled in, thinking about the small bit of rice we'd eaten two days before. "It's been a while."

She hugged me. "Okay. Okay, that's all over now. Nathan?"

"I'm on it," he said before leaving the room.

After a couple of minutes, he returned with two sandwiches. Halle and I grabbed them from his hands before immediately chomping into them. I thought that I would have to ask for another one, but by the time I took the last bite, I was full.

Nathan handed us each a glass of water, and we gulped it down. Halle wiped her mouth with her wrist.

"Okay," Mom said. "Time to wash."

We stood outside and peeled off our clothes. They were so dirty that they were stiff. Mom was on her knees, using rags and a basin to scrub Halle, and I washed myself. I was more concerned with getting clean and washing the awful summer off of me than being undressed outside.

Several graves were under the tree, and Mom glanced behind her.

"Dr. Hayes, his girlfriend, and our friend Cooper," she said. "He was Ashley's boyfriend. Remember her? She's Dr. Hayes's daughter."

"Her boyfriend died?" I asked.

Mom pulled her mouth to the side. "Saving Zoe. That's the little girl in there. She's Nathan's daughter. And Elleny is the other little girl."

"Is she Nathan's daughter, too?" Halle asked.

Mom poured a little water over Halle's head and then lathered bar soap in her hands. She scrubbed Halle's hair until it was blonde again. She shook her head. "She found us."

"The big guy was our neighbor in Shallot," I said.

"Skeeter?" Mom said, her eyebrows shooting up.

"That's Skeeter? I wish I'd known. He lived a few houses down from us in Shallot."

She paused. "Wait. What do you mean?"

"I saw you." I dried off and pulled an oversized but clean T-shirt over my head. "Your whole group, the day you left with Skeeter. I didn't know it was you though."

Mom shook her head, her eyes falling to the concrete patio we were sitting on. "You were right there?"

I nodded.

She closed her eyes tight. "So, you were there this whole time? And last night when we spent the night?"

"Joey came into our house," Halle said. "When he found out it was us, he was going to bring us to you, but he got bit, so we stayed inside."

Mom covered her mouth and listened while Halle recounted our entire ordeal—from the moment Dad had picked her up from school until we'd reached the top of the red dirt hill.

"Jesus," Mom said, shaking her head, her hand trembling. She closed her eyes and then took a deep breath, willing it away. "Joey was a good man. It makes sense that he tried to save you. I'm so sorry about your dad."

"Mom?" I said. "We didn't leave him."

"What do you mean?"

"He was bitten. He got really sick, and..." I trailed off, unable to say the words.

"Oh no. No, no, no..."

At first, I thought she was disappointed in me, and then she wrapped me in her arms and squeezed.

"I'm so sorry you had to do that, Jenna. My God, you are so brave." She sucked in a faltering breath. "You're here now, and we're together. I know that your dad would be so proud of you for that."

Once Halle was dressed in her own oversized T-shirt, Mom walked us to the table and let us eat again. This time, it was canned peaches. We practically inhaled them, and then we each drank another glass of water.

With full bellies, we were guided into Mom's room, and she turned down the covers.

"You've had a long day."

We climbed into bed and settled in.

Halle gripped her fingers tightly around Mom's wrist. "Don't leave, Mommy."

She shook her head, brought Halle's hand to her mouth, and gave it a kiss. "We'll never be apart again."

"You promise?" Halle asked.

"I *promise*. You are so brave," Mom said before kissing Halle's forehead. Then, she looked into my eyes and touched my cheek. "So brave."

Mom sat in a chair in the corner of the room while Halle and I lay quietly, waiting to fall asleep. She stared at us as I stared at her. I was almost afraid to close my eyes. I was afraid I would wake up in Shallot, and it would all be a dream.

I had spent the last four months with one goal in mind. Now that we were finally with Mom, after fighting so hard and surviving so much, the fear that it would never happen was replaced with the fear that it would be taken away.

Soon though, my eyes grew heavy, and I drifted off to sleep. The last forty-eight hours replayed, swallowing me, and then spit me out into the halls of Bishop Middle School where I was giggling with my classmates and teachers and then waving to my dad as he arrived to pick me up after school in his dress blues. This time though, Mom was with him, and I knew everything would be all right.

My eyes peeled open, and I blinked. The sun was pouring in through the top half of the window, and I reached over for Halle, feeling nothing but wrinkled sheets and a pillow.

I sat up fast, my heart slamming against my chest in a panic. My shoulders relaxed when I saw Mom watching me from her chair with Halle curled up asleep in her lap.

"Good morning," she cooed.

I sighed and then lay back down, my head propped by the pillow. "Oh, thank God."

Mom smiled. "I know. I woke up afraid it was just a dream, too. But you're here, and I'm here, and we're all okay."

"Is everyone still asleep?" I asked.

She shook her head. "The boys are outside, burying Miranda and Bryce. We're going to have a little funeral when Ashley feels up to it."

"Miranda was her sister," I said, more of a statement than a question.

"Yes," Mom said.

"Do those cars outside have gas?" I asked.

"A little. Why?"

"We left people behind in Fairview about a month ago. They have little kids there, toddlers, younger than Halle. I was hoping, if we had enough gas, we could go get them."

"I'll talk to the others. I bet we can."

I breathed out a long breath of relief. "Things have been bad for so long. It feels strange for it to be okay."

"I know."

"I just wish Dad were here."

"I know you do, honey. I'm so sorry. I'm *so* sorry. I can't imagine how hard that was for you and how hard it's been for you, being alone and taking care of Halle."

"I can't explain it."

"If you ever want to try, I'm always here to listen."

"I know," I said.

A quiet knock sounded on the door.

"Come in," Mom said softly. "Hi, Elleny. This is Jenna, my oldest."

"Hi," Elleny said with a reserved grin. "I've heard a lot about you."

She reminded me of Chloe, and I remembered how much I missed my friend.

"Nate said Ashley's ready."

Mom nodded and then shook Halle gently awake, kissing her temple. "Baby girl, it's time to wake up."

"What?" Halle said, looking around with wide eyes.

Mom helped Halle put on her glasses. "Hi," Mom said, smiling.

Halle threw her arms around Mom's neck. "Mommy!"

Mom closed her eyes tight and hugged her back. "We've got to go outside and say good-bye to our friends. Will you come outside with me?"

Halle climbed down off of Mom's lap, and then we followed her and Elleny outside in our bare feet. The T-shirt I wore was nearly to my knees, and Halle's shirt almost dragged against the ground. Our clothes were still drying from when Nathan had washed them the night before.

Ashley, Nathan, Zoe, and Skeeter were standing next to two fresh mounds of dirt.

Ashley's eyes were swollen and red, but she smiled when she saw Halle and me. "Hi, girls," she whispered.

I mirrored her expression, but I knew exactly how she felt, and I questioned how she could do anything but cry. Then, my eyes drifted to the other graves. Her father was buried there, and so was her boyfriend. I wondered if there was a point when loss stopped hurting so much. Maybe she was just used to the pain, or maybe we were a distraction.

Nathan spoke about Miranda and Bryce and about how they'd died saving Halle and me, and then everyone told funny stories about them. Ashley, Nathan, and Zoe put flowers on each of the graves, and then we walked to the porch, everyone finding a seat.

"It feels strange to sit out here and not watch the hill for the girls," Mom said. She was sitting between us and hugged us both to each of her sides.

The wheat waved in the cool morning breeze, hissing gently in harmony with wind blowing through the trees. Mom rested her cheek on my head as Halle climbed onto her lap. A peaceful expression on her face hinted at utter bliss. We had finally found her. When she reached over and intertwined her fingers with Nathan's, I knew that we had completed the happiness that she'd somehow found at the end of the world.

the end

THANK YOU for reading *Among Monsters*! This was a difficult and deeply personal novel for me to write, and I'm so thankful that you let me share it with you.

acknowledgments

THERE ARE TWO KINDS OF AUTHORS—those who make plenty of time for a release, gliding in with everything in place weeks prior, and then those who are flying one hundred miles per hour toward release day by the seat of their pants with windblown hair and a missing earring. Thank you to my publicist, Autumn Hull; editor/formatter, Jovana Shirley; and cover designer, Sarah Hansen, for not quitting on me for being the latter.

Thank you to Danielle Lagasse, Kelli Spear, and Jessica Landers for leading one hell of a good group of strong women (and three men). The MacPack is an enormous group, and you three manage to keep it clean, keep it positive, keep it real, and keep it focused even if that means you have to be the bad guys once in a while. I am forever grateful to you and the members for being so supportive and keeping a smile on my face on the tough days.

Thank you to author Eden Fierce for inspiring and consulting on the character of Jenna and for helping me with some of the teacher's names. I know you included them because they mean something special to you.

That said, thank you to Mrs. Stuckey, Mr. Hilterbran, and Mrs. Siders for making a difference.

Thank you to Chloe-Beth for the use of your name!

Thank you to Miss Katy for keeping Babyspawn busy while I'm writing and wearing the many hats of a writer.

Thank you to my husband for being understanding about sleeping alone most nights when I'm writing against a deadline.

Thank you to author Teresa Mummert. Some days, quite honestly, I feel like you've kept me sane. You keep me strong. You keep me smiling. You keep me focused on what is important. Thank you for being a best friend.

about the author

JAMIE MCGUIRE was born in Tulsa, Oklahoma. She attended Northern Oklahoma College, the University of Central Oklahoma, and Autry Technology Center where she graduated with a degree in Radiography.

Jamie paved the way for the New Adult genre with the international bestseller, *Beautiful Disaster*. Her follow-up novel *Walking Disaster* debuted at #1 on the *New York Times*, *USA Today*, and *Wall Street Journal* bestseller lists. *Beautiful Oblivion*, book one of the Maddox Brothers books, also topped the *New York Times* bestseller list, debuting at #1. She has also written apocalyptic thriller *Red Hill*; the Providence series, a young adult paranormal romance trilogy; and several novellas, including *A Beautiful Wedding*, *Among Monsters: A Red Hill Novella*, and *Happenstance: A Novella Series*.

Jamie lives on a ranch just outside Enid, Oklahoma, with her husband, Jeff, and their three children. They share their thirty acres with cattle, six horses, three dogs, and Rooster the cat.

Find Jamie at www.jamiemcguire.com or on Facebook, Twitter, and Instagram!

Made in United States
North Haven, CT
26 November 2023